MAIN ROAD SURGERY

With Dr Ann Davis's adoptive parents going to live abroad, the way is clear for her to seek out her natural mother—a move her adoptive mother has long feared. To commence her search, Ann enters General Practice in a town little known to her. Hurdles present themselves from the outset, not only in her quest, but in her personal life too, so that she begins to question the wisdom of her actions ...

MAIN ROAD SURGERY

To adopted children.
If you seek at all,
Seek selflessly.

MAIN ROAD SURGERY

by

Frances Fitzgibbon

Dales Large Print Books
Long Preston, North Yorkshire,
England.

British Library Cataloguing in Publication Data.

Fitzgibbon, Frances
 Main Road Surgery.

 A catalogue record for this book is
 available from the British Library

 ISBN 1-85389-952-6 pbk

First published in Great Britain by Robert Hale Ltd., 1983

Copyright © 1983 by Frances Fitzgibbon

Cover illustration © Behrens by arrangement with Allied Artists

The moral right of the author has been asserted

Published in Large Print 1999 by arrangement with Robert Hale Ltd.

Dales Large Print is an imprint of
Library Magna Books Ltd.
Printed and bound in Great Britain by
T.J. International Ltd., Cornwall, PL28 8RW.

ONE

Ann Davis tossed her white coat on to the back seat of her car and turning on the engine, made her way through the wide exit gates of St Mark's Hospital.

The March sunshine with its promise of spring weather, lifted her spirits and warmed her heart after the bitter winter.

Reaching her parents' home on the outskirts of the city, she turned her blue Mini off the road and into the gravel drive. Stepping out of the car, she looked up at the lovely old house and thought how much she'd miss these regular trips home.

Pushing open the glass-panelled front door, the first thing she saw standing in the hall were the suitcases. She'd been about to call out 'Hello Mum, Dad', the way she always did on her arrival home, but the words died on her lips. It was only in that moment that the full impact of her parents departure really descended upon her.

Almost immediately, she crushed the self-indulgent, piteous thoughts and trying to adopt a cheerful note, called 'Hello Mum, Dad.'

'That you, Ann, darling?' came her mother's voice from somewhere upstairs.

Simultaneously, the lounge door opened to reveal her father.

'Ann dear.' His face broke into a welcoming smile.

'You've made it.' He came towards her and putting an arm round her shoulder, drew her into the lounge.

'Ohh!' Iris Davis moaned, coming into the room and collapsing into an armchair. 'Never again.' She stretched out and closed her eyes. 'As if the packing wasn't bad enough without having to leave the place shipshape.'

'I told you, Mum. You needn't have ...'

'I know, darling. I know. But how could I leave it all to you? It would be different if Jane was here to help.'

Ann laughed. 'Anyway, it's all behind you now and ...'

'Behind me! But now I've got the flight to face. Eleven hours!'

Frank Davis smiled at his wife and shook his head. 'Iris, you are quite impossible.'

'But Mum,' Ann reminded her, 'you've flown abroad for holidays for years.'

'You're right I guess,' her mother said resignedly. 'I suppose I'm really all churned up at leaving you behind.' She looked despairingly at her daughter.

'Now Iris,' her husband admonished lightly, 'after all these years you surely ...'

'But you know how I am about things,' she cut him off. 'Even after all these years that woman could ...'

'*That woman,* as you insist on calling

her,' Frank Davis reasoned, 'gave up any rights to her child twenty-six years ago. You surely ...'

'Look, Mum,' Ann intervened, 'You are the only parents I have ever known. Nothing can change that. You will always be my mother, the same as Dad here will always be my father.'

Her mother was silent for a moment, eyes closed, biting her bottom lip. 'Promise me, Ann ...'

'Iris!' Frank said firmly. 'It's not fair to extract promises.'

'Promise me,' Iris went on, ignoring his remark, 'if that woman should ever find you, you won't listen to her—you won't forsake me.'

'Mum!' Ann objected vehemently, getting up and moving to the window. 'How can you even *think* such a thing?'

'Leave it, Iris! For God's sake, leave it!' Frank pleaded.

'I'm sorry.' There was a catch in her voice. 'I really hadn't meant to spoil this last evening together.'

Taking the cue, Ann turned brightly from the window, 'Who's for a sherry before dinner?'

So the subject was closed, but not without causing Ann a great deal of inner turmoil. Perhaps James was right after all. Perhaps it *was* wrong of her to think of tracing her natural mother. But it was this very attitude of her adoptive mother towards her natural mother, that had initially aroused her curiosity. What was there that she didn't want Ann to know? What was it that she feared?

All too soon it was time to leave for the airport some fifteen miles away.

'Seems such a shame your sister couldn't be here,' Iris lamented.

'Air fares from Bermuda cost money,' Frank reasoned. 'It's not a commodity that husband of hers has to spare.'

'And it is only three months since she was here,' Ann comforted, recalling sadly how her sister's attitude towards her had not improved as a result of their separation.

'You're right of course,' Iris agreed. 'I do wish we were going by taxi,' she said as they loaded the luggage into Ann's car. 'I hate the thought of you out on these roads after dark.'

'What about when I go into the outside world and have to answer night calls?' her daughter wanted to know.

'I'll *never* be happy about you driving. Day or night.'

'Oh, Mum! You should learn to drive then you wouldn't worry.'

'Never!' Iris shuddered. 'Never!'

'Iris, love.' Her husband put a protective arm about her. 'Don't worry so.'

Ann looked at her parents standing there in a pool of light thrown out from the house and thought how much she owed them and how much she was going to miss them.

The departure lounge was cold and draughty and the coffee served in paper cups was only lukewarm and bitter. It did nothing to settle Ann's churning stomach, though outwardly she appeared calm and composed.

Frank Davis was craning his neck, head to one side, listening to the announcement of the flight call.

'That's ours, Iris.'

'Oh, my child,' she sobbed, wrapping her arms around her daughter.

'Come on, Mum,' Ann soothed, struggling to keep back the lump which was threatening to choke her. 'You mustn't miss your flight.'

She felt her father's firm hand on her shoulder and gently eased herself from her mother's embrace.

'Well, Ann,' her father was saying, 'keep us posted on your love life and don't work *too* hard.' Then as his wife moved away to pick up her small piece of hand luggage, he pulled his daughter to him and hugged her, then taking his wife by the hand he led her away.

Iris Davis, with her head turned, kept her gaze fixed on her daughter's face until the gathering fellow passengers no longer made it possible.

Soon, Ann could not distinguish her parents from the crowd, so turning away, she left the terminal buildings and crossed to the car park.

Despite the feeling of emptiness, of loss at her mother and father's departure, Ann could not altogether suppress the tiny bubble of excitement, of anticipation, that until now she had restrained so successfully.

At last she was free to seek out her natural mother. With four thousand miles to be soon between them, there could be no risk of any discovery on her part threatening the relationship with her adoptive parents. She had promised herself long since that she would spare them any hurt.

Perhaps her mind was elsewhere as she left the car park, perhaps she even glanced skywards for a fleeting second, but when she felt the jarring bump, she'd no idea what had happened. With a sound of breaking glass her car came to a standstill.

Her stomach lurched and her heart began to race as she became aware of her misdemeanour. Quite unknowingly, she had come so close to the line of parked cars on her left, that she had actually hit one. What was even worse, there was someone in it, or there had been until now.

A tall, lean figure of a man had climbed out and was bending over to inspect the damage.

She was shaking too violently to trust herself to get out, so leaning over her passenger seat, she wound down her window.

'I'm t-t-terribly sorry,' she stuttered. 'It was my fault.' Almost immediately, she recalled her father's advice never to admit blame.

'I should think so too,' drawled the lean stranger, turning from his inspection and stooping to gaze in on her. 'You got something against me, coming straight at me like that?'

She didn't miss the amusement in his voice despite the seriousness of the matter.

'I'm sorry,' she rushed on, still shaken. 'I've no idea how ... oh dear ...' She couldn't check the quiver in her voice and the tears which threatened to overwhelm her.

'Steady on. Steady on,' he said calmly, with no intimation of the anger she would have been feeling had their roles been reversed. 'Nothing very serious about a smashed headlight. Luckily the bulb's still intact but we'd better exchange names and addresses just the same. You stay right where you are.' He then got into his car and reversed a few feet leaving her plenty of clearance for driving away.

'Thank you, Ma'am" he drawled a few moments later as they exchanged slips of paper. He banged lightly on her car bodywork. 'Mind how you go.'

Ann was back at St Mark's before her tension eased and she found herself laughing remembering the stranger's easy manner and she congratulated herself on such a thin escape.

It was two days later while half expecting a letter requesting the name of her insurers that the other letter arrived. As soon as she saw the postmark her hands trembled in her eagerness to open it.

She knew how the contents could very well decide her future. Standing there in the Common Room in the presence of her colleagues, she became acutely conscious of the need to open this letter in privacy so slipping out, made her way to her room.

With her present job at St Mark's coming to a close, for some months she had been scanning the 'posts available' column in the medical journals, uncertain still which line of medicine to pursue.

Then, when she'd made an application for this particular post, things had miraculously begun to fall into place. Her way had suddenly become crystal clear.

When she had been short-listed for interview, she had told no-one except James. Totally opposed to her idea, he had gone so far as to say that he hoped she would be unsuccessful.

Remembering the gruelling interview now, her hopes were far from high as with unsteady hands, she used her nailfile to slit open the envelope.

Her eyes flew over the typed sheet, excitement mounting as she read and re-read the one sentence which said all she needed to know.

We would be happy therefore if you could take up your appointment at Main Road Surgery, Hargate, on the morning of the first of April.

The letter then went on to say that in the event of her declining this offer, the partners would appreciate an immediate reply.

There had of course been other interviews for other posts, one even here at

St Mark's but they faded instantly into oblivion, as with increasing certainty, Ann knew that this letter clinched her decision, once and for all.

She got up from where she'd been sitting and crossed the small room to her desk. Opening the right-hand drawer she lifted out a thick folder of lecture notes. Her hands now steady, she then picked up the brown envelope lying there and slid out the enclosed certificate.

Unfolding the slightly yellowing form with its red printing, she read yet again, the scant but vital information.

It stated, in even black handwriting that a female, Kathleen Ann, had been born to one Kathleen Morgan on the thirty-first of December 1955, at 3 Mount Street, Hargate.

Now that same female, renamed Ann Louise by her adoptive parents, was to return as Doctor Davis to the place of her birth, where the quest for her natural mother could at last begin.

Ann closed her eyes momentarily and prayed silently that what she was about to set out to do, would bring harm to no one as James had tried to infer.

There was no sunshine filtering into the wards today, but the dull grey weather did little to dampen Ann's excitement as she almost flew around carrying out her duties.

'Your parents get off all right?' her friend, Sister June Row wanted to know.

'Yes, thanks. They'll be soaking up the Kenyan sun by now.'

'I think I'd die,' June lamented, 'if my parents decided to go and live at the other side of the globe.'

'It's not quite like that,' Ann reasoned. 'But with Dad's firm closing down and his old colleague starting up in East Africa ... well ... it's not everybody gets a chance of a partnership like that.'

She didn't go on to tell June of her appointment in Hargate yet and knew it was only because she was uneasy about telling James.

At thirty, he was young to be Hospital Secretary which only served to draw emphasis to his qualities of management and public relations.

After arriving at St Mark's, Ann had several professional dealings with James Divine but their first social encounter had been at the Annual Hospital Dinner. This had led to her accompanying him to other formal gatherings and from these, their relationship had developed.

This evening he was taking her out to dinner to a quiet restaurant just out of the city which they often frequented now. His white Cortina estate was parked in the spot reserved for him and she saw it as she left the hospital building.

He must have been watching for her, as his car door opened immediately and he made his way to meet her, immaculately turned out as always.

'Everything all right?'

Instantly, Ann was irritated recognizing in his tone that which she'd heard him use around the hospital corridors, to staff and visitors alike.

'Of course. Shouldn't it be?'

He took her arm. 'I thought you might be a bit down after your parents' departure.'

Directly she was sorry. He was only concerned for her and knew no other way of expressing it. In sharp contrast, an image of the lean stranger at the airport flashed before her mind. She had planned to tell James of the incident, but guessing his disapproval at her carelessness and the man's familiarity, she decided against it.

'I don't think it has hit me yet that Mum and Dad are no longer here,' she said brightly, getting into the car.

'I suppose not.' He shut her door and went round to his side. 'Any news on the job front yet?'

'In here.' She patted her handbag and smiled nervously.

'Come on then. Tell all.' He turned towards her expectantly. 'I hope it's at St Mark's.'

'Let's get away from here first.' She looked out at the busy car park.

'All right.' He started the engine and drove off.

Ann waited until they were seated at a quiet corner table in the peaceful restaurant and until they had placed their order, before, taking the letter from her handbag, she passed it silently to James.

She studied his smooth face as his eyes moved over the paper and then watched, as the lines of his mouth became firmer.

'You're going ahead with it then?' he said finally, without meeting her eyes.

'Don't you see I have to now?' she appealed to him.

'No. I don't, Ann. I don't see that at all.' Very slowly, he folded up the letter and handed it back to her. 'It's not too late to turn it down.'

'But I don't want to, James. This is the job I wanted. More than all the others put together.'

'For all the wrong reasons,' he said

steadily. 'You've not begun to consider the implications ... the heartbreak you could cause ... the ...'

'Oh but I have, James. You know I have. I've not gone into this lightly ... not from the very beginning.' She fell silent as the waiter came with the soup.

When he'd gone, leaning across the table, James began again. 'Besides this crazy notion of searching out your roots, as you put it, have you thought what you're turning your back on?'

'Very carefully.'

They ate their soup in silence. All the while the waiter served the main course neither looked at each other, both lost in their own thoughts.

At last James broke the silence. 'You're turning your back on a whole way of life ... your friends and colleagues, your familiar surroundings, your home. And me.'

'But Hargate is only twenty miles away, James,' she argued, growing impatient yet knowing that all he was saying was true.

'And why you? What difference will it make to us?'

'A new life, new contacts ... you'll see.' He fell silent, left his food and gazed past her, his eyes unseeing.

Ann no longer felt hungry and only toyed with her food from then on. Soft background music did little to quell her disturbed emotions. She no longer knew what to say, to impress upon him the importance to her of pursuing this quest on which she had set her heart.

After a long period of silence during which she poured coffee, James finally moved an arm across the table and covered her small hand with one of his.

'Ann,' he began in a tone of hushed urgency, 'would you ... would you call the whole thing off if ... if I asked you to marry me?'

She felt no rising excitement, no shared intimacy at this unexpected question, nothing except sadness that he should choose this moment to ask her. She had no hesitation in replying.

'I'm accepting this post at Hargate, James. I'm going through with my search.' Gently, she moved her hand from under his. She made no reference to his conditional proposal for she felt it would have been erroneous to do so.

TWO

James remained critical of and totally opposed to Ann's decision, but nevertheless insisted on driving her to Hargate to see over two flats.

They were entering the small town when they discovered that traffic was being diverted due to a burst main and they found themselves having to make quite a detour to reach their destination.

'James!' Ann exclaimed suddenly. 'Please stop.'

'I can't just here.' He glanced in his overhead mirror. 'There's a whole stream of traffic on my tail.'

'Well pull in or *something.*' Her voice had risen in agitation.

'Whatever's wrong?' he demanded, when he was finally able to stop.

'Back there!' She turned and pointed excitedly. 'The first opening past the telephone kiosk.'

'What is it, Ann?'

'It's Mount Street, James. *Mount* Street!' She wanted him to hurry yet was half afraid at the same time.

'Look, Ann ...'

'Please, James! If you don't turn round I shall just get out and walk back.' She had one hand on the door handle.

'Stay where you are. I'll take you, but what exactly do you intend doing?'

'Let's just drive past for now.' Waves of apprehension were washing over her.

Turning onto an old, uneven road surface, they saw that the properties in Mount Street were Victorian terrace houses.

James stopped the car. 'You absolutely sure you know what you're doing?' he asked, disapproval heavy in his voice.

'Oh yes. Absolutely.' She wound down her window. 'That's number ninety-seven.

We want to be right at the other end.'
Excitement was mounting in her voice.

With a final glance her way, James shook his head and pulled away. The street curved sharply and beyond the curve, James slowed down at the scene suddenly revealed and pulled in to the side of the road.

Ann gasped, a hand raised to her mouth. 'I don't believe it.'

'Well! That puts an end to that!' He began to reverse as if in preparation to make a three-point turn.

'Wait!' Ann snapped, putting a hand on his arm.

'What's the point?' He turned towards her, then leaning over peered through her window at the number on the end house. 'Forty-nine that side.' He then wound his own window down. 'Fifty this side.'

'You needn't sound so pleased about it,' she accused in a choked voice.

'That's hardly fair, Ann.'

'Please drive on to the end,' she

requested in a small voice.

So they drove on, past the stretch of waste land where remnants of demolition were still scattered about and then on past a block of new flats, some still in the process of being built.

'That's it then,' James said. 'Your search ended before it began.'

'Oh no,' Ann said with increased determination. 'I'll find her now if it's the very last thing I ever do.'

James made no reply to her impassioned outburst, but Ann knew from the whiteness of his knuckles on the steering-wheel, that it was taking all his self-control to remain silent.

For her part she was still too stunned to take in much of Hargate from then on, until James brought the car to a standstill alongside a tree-fringed area of grassland which stretched towards the town.

Slowly, Ann looked about her, from the gracious Victorian buildings on one side of the road, to the clusters of golden daffodils standing tall beneath the line of giant trees on the other.

'It's quite lovely here,' she said in a hushed voice.

'Reasonably pleasant,' James admitted grudgingly.

She looked towards the tall houses, then flung open the car door and climbed out. 'Coming?'

With markedly less enthusiasm, James got out of the car and after locking his door, went carefully round checking each of the others.

They crossed the road in silence. Ann, now very aware of her surroundings, inhaled deeply. 'Mmm,' she murmured with pleasure, 'isn't this lovely after the noise and fumes of the city?'

'Can't imagine much going on here,' he remarked disparagingly as they mounted the steps to the front door of a spacious old house.

When they emerged half an hour later, Ann's face was alight, while James's mouth, set in a thin line, told of his disapproval.

'You could have asked her to wait a day or two while you made up your mind,' he objected.

'My mind *is* made up, James. Besides, I don't think I'd find a nicer flat.' They were back at the car now and cool though it still was, Ann had a sudden urge to kick off her shoes and run barefoot in the grass. She was just about to say as much to James when she felt his eyes upon her. Seeing his stony expression and the car door held open for her, she knew he would consider her crazy if she were to suggest such a thing.

'Hargate's not a very big town,' he said seriously, once seated behind the steering-wheel.

'I know that, James.' She was surprised by his remark.

'And you *are* coming here as a General Practitioner.'

'Yes?' She was puzzled now.

'Has it occurred to you that you'll hardly

be incognito? You start asking questions,' his voice rose in disquiet, 'and God knows what people will think.'

'Please give me a little more credit than that, James,' she said with practised patience, looking straight ahead.

'But you could be risking your position. You could ...'

'So you think my illegitimacy could affect my social status, do you?' she snapped, impatient now, without mercy.

'It's not just that,' he argued. 'But people do talk and who knows what it might lead to?'

'Will you please shut up!' Ann's voice was dangerously calm. Coming across Mount Street like that and then finding number three had been demolished, had been a big enough blow without having to listen to James pontificate like this.

'I'm sorry.' He sighed. 'Come to Hargate if you must, but I do wish you'd call off this search for your mother.'

'Let's find somewhere to eat,' she

suggested, carefully ignoring his request.

They were lucky enough to get a window seat in the first-floor Chicken Bar of an hotel overlooking the wide stretches of open grassland, undoubtedly the town's greatest attraction.

The branches of the sturdy old trees were still bare though Ann knew, despite the encroaching dusk, if she were to peer closer, she would find those branches covered with millions of buds with their promise of summer splendour.

'There are a few things from home I shall bring to the flat,' Ann said.

'Good thing I have an estate car.'

'Oh, you mustn't feel ...'

'I can hardly leave you to shift stuff on your own. Besides, your Mini won't take that much.'

'Well actually, Uncle John has offered to move anything over. Which reminds me,' Ann went on, 'I'm going out to the farm for lunch on Sunday. Aunt Brenda invited you too.'

'This Sunday?'

'Yes. Is something wrong?'

'It's this coming weekend I'm going home. You did say some time ago, you may come with me ...?'

'Oh dear!' Ann had just picked up her coffee cup and replaced it instantly in the saucer. 'I'd quite forgotten. I am sorry.'

'My parents must be beginning to think there's something wrong with you. Every time ...'

'Look, James! I've said I'm sorry.' She lowered her voice, conscious that heads were turned in their direction. 'Why is it that we seem to do nothing but argue just lately?'

'It's only since you adopted this notion of coming to live here,' he reasoned. 'That and this other crazy notion.'

Ann gripped the edges of the table. 'Once and for all, will you *please* stop going on so.'

Driving back to the city, Ann felt had

she been on her own today and found her mother's home no longer standing, she'd have rushed straight to the Housing Department in an effort to discover where the occupants had moved to.

James was right of course about the difficulty of her being free to make enquiries incognito. It wouldn't be long in a town this size, before her blue Mini was recognized as 'the doctor's car'. She'd been foolish to believe she could retain her anonymity in such a place.

Next morning there was a letter from her mother, the first since she would have received news of Ann's appointment in Hargate.

Send us some photos of the Surgery. Sorry you won't be living at home but find a nice flat. Your father's business is taking up most of his time. I'm helping at a school for the deaf and playing bridge and may even take up golf ...

Ann read the letter twice. She was

pleased to learn that her parents were settling and adapting to their new life so quickly.

Hargate of course would mean nothing to her parents for they had never seen Ann's original birth certificate. The social worker who she had talked with before gaining access to the certificate, had pointed out that adoptive parents would not be given such information, though they would be quite likely to be told a little of the mother's circumstances and what her job was.

There was another letter that day, bearing a Hargate postmark. On opening it she was surprised to find a printed invitation card to the Hargate Medical Society Annual Dinner for Friday of that week. A brief, handwritten note was enclosed from Doctor A. Clarke, the retiring partner in the practice, who she was replacing.

Good opportunity to meet the local medics. No need to reply. Shall look out for you by the main door at seven.

Ann couldn't help smiling at what seemed to her a kind of royal summons, yet she knew old Doctor Clarke had made this move with only her good in mind. Providing she could swap her on-call she would go.

Ann parked her car in front of the Crown Hotel in Hargate just a few minutes before seven and flicked a comb through her soft curls. Unsure of how formal or informal it would be, she'd chosen to wear a soft blue, woollen dress and wore over it, her dark blue velvet jacket.

A few couples were trickling in through the main door as she approached and she noticed the men wore bow ties.

'Doctor Davis!' The kind-faced elderly gentleman stepped out in front of her as soon as Ann crossed the threshold. He turned towards the white-haired woman by his side. 'This is the young woman, Nancy, who's stepping into my shoes.'

Then turning back to Ann. 'My wife, Mrs Clarke.'

Moving forward, the woman extended a hand to their young guest. 'Welcome to Hargate, my dear, and where are you going to be living?'

Ann told her as they followed Doctor Clarke past the reception area into a small bar where people were standing around talking. Several heads turned in their direction and Ann felt herself falling under scrutiny.

'Always causes a stir when we've a newcomer in our midst.' Doctor Clarke raised one bushy eyebrow and his face lit up with obvious delight. 'Specially one as pretty as you. Come and meet Currie and Murdie. Sound like a pair of gangsters, eh?' He headed towards a small group.

'Hi there!' The tall, younger one of the two greeted her while eyeing her appraisingly.

'Good evening,' the other said quietly, nodding towards her with a slow smile.

'Good evening,' Ann replied, moving into the small circle opened up to admit the newcomers.

Then, despite the efforts of Nancy Clarke to steer the talk away from medicine, it wasn't long before the problems of the practice were being discussed.

'The work load's doubled since this chap arrived with his new-fangled ways,' Doctor Clarke complained.

'Nevertheless, I think he's got the right idea,' Doctor Murdie suggested.

'The patients certainly think so,' Doctor Currie agreed in a quiet voice.

'We've a new consultant surgeon at the local hospital,' Doctor Clarke explained to Ann. 'Sends all his patients home far too early and expects *us* to take over.'

'Don't colour her judgement so, Arthur,' Nancy Clarke reproached her husband. She turned to Ann. 'He's speaking tonight, dear, so you can form your own judgement.'

Ann was denied the chance of replying

as the call to be seated for dinner went out just then. She was placed between Doctor and Mrs Clarke and while he was involved in deep conversation with someone on his left, his wife questioned Ann about her family. Nancy Clarke showed particular interest in her parents being in Kenya, a country it seemed she had always wanted to visit.

'Perhaps when Arthur's played every golf course in the British Isles, I'll get him to try those in Kenya.'

'What's that, Nancy?' her husband intervened just then.

While she explained, Ann let her eyes travel round the room at the other guests. It was when she reached the top table that her attention was suddenly arrested.

A tall, lean man with dark hair, face full of laughter was listening attentively to something his companion was saying. She was an extremely attractive blonde and had her face turned up towards his.

Where had she seen the man before?

Even while she watched him, she felt his eyes glance in her direction. She looked away flustered, yet not before she had seen the almost imperceptible tilt of his head towards her, as if in subtle acknowledgement.

Then someone was banging on the table praying silence for Mr Iain Kirk. The name of course was the same as on that piece of paper he'd given her out at the airport that night.

'Doctors—ladies—and gentlemen!' began the tall lean man rising to his feet, in a voice immediately recognizable to Ann.

All sound in the room died away and heads turned in his direction. Someone cleared their throat and he waited before going on. Ann tried desperately to relax her tense body.

'It gives me great pleasure to have this opportunity of speaking with you all tonight.' He looked slowly and deliberately along the tables and Ann let her eyes fall. 'There are faces I know,' he paused, 'and faces I don't know. I am aware of the misgivings of some of you in general practice about my ...'

'Here here,' someone muttered and banged on the table.

'... about my policies,' he went on undeterred. 'But I would like to emphasize, that any extra work load can be more than justified, by the knowledge that the waiting list has been more than halved.'

There were a few murmurs round the room, some sanctioning his words, others obviously not.

'Isn't he gorgeous,' Nancy Clarke whispered in Ann's ear. 'No wonder he's the local heart-throb.'

Ann only smiled reservedly by way of answer, while Doctor Clarke peered at the speaker disapprovingly over the top of his spectacles.

In the after-dinner socializing, she was acutely aware of his presence, and when Sean Murdie suggested she might like to be introduced to Iain Kirk, she made the feeble excuse that it was time she was getting back to St Mark's.

In her work as a G.P. in the town, Ann knew she would be certain to come up against him fairly frequently and remembering the incident at the airport, she couldn't expect him to rate her very highly.

She was already up and dressed by nine o'clock on Sunday when her Uncle John arrived as promised in his station wagon, to transport her belongings from the hospital room to her new flat.

'You said you might want to call round home?' he prompted as he put the last of her boxes into his vehicle.

'Yes. There are a few things I'd like to pick up.'

'Can't say I'm altogether happy about your father leaving that place empty.'

'But it's all well locked up, Uncle John.'

'Maybe. Nevertheless ...'

'And the neighbours keep an eye.'

'All the same, it'll maybe be a good thing if Jane does come home.'

'Jane?'

'Hasn't your aunt told you?' He was in his van now fastening his safety belt.

'Told me what?' she asked, standing alongside.

'She had a letter from Jane. It seems she's talking about the possibilities of coming back in the summer.'

'But what about Rick's job?'

'On her own I understand.' He looked askance at his niece.

'Surely ...'

'Don't know any more than that.' He switched on the engine. 'Best get on now.'

Some time later, as they pushed open the door of the farmhouse, delicious aromas of home baking greeted them.

'We're back, Brenda,' John Davis called before stomping up the stairs. 'You go through, Ann, I'll just change and get back out to me work.'

45

'Now then, Ann.' Her aunt, red-faced and hands in flour looked up and smiled broadly. 'Everything all right?'

'Fine thanks.' She looked appreciatively at the well-laden cooling trays. 'Gosh! Anyone would think you were feeding an army.'

'Well. Jack and his family arrive to-morrow.'

'Uncle John never said.'

'Ah well.' Aunt Brenda dropped her voice. 'You know how he is.'

'Still?'

'Oh, he's accepted it, and they get on.' She paused and listened. 'I thought that was him.' She went back to rolling pastry. 'It still doesn't stop him being sore that his only son chose banking as a career.'

'You can understand that of course,' Ann reasoned, crossing to the sink where dishes were piled waiting to be washed.

'Will you come away from there?' her aunt demanded,

'Not likely. Do you think I'm going to stand and watch while ...'

'You two arguing already?' John Davis came into the room and stooped to kiss his wife. 'I'll be off then, love.'

'Lunch for one,' she reminded him.

'I'll be here.' Then he was gone, the door banging shut behind him.

There was a momentary silence in the kitchen and Ann turned to find her aunt standing looking after her husband.

'He's a good man, but a proud one,' she said more to herself than to Ann. 'Different kind of pride to what that young man of yours shows mind.'

'You don't like James do you, Aunt?'

'Now I never said as much, did I?'

'No,' Ann agreed. 'Not quite.'

'Well then. But to get back to your uncle. He thinks because his father farmed here and his grandfather before him, that so it should continue.' She opened the oven door and stood back from the heat before going on. 'Much the same way as

47

you've gone in for medicine,' she said matter-of-factly.

'How do you mean?' Ann was puzzled.

'Well with your own mother being a nurse. Same line of ...'

'Mum? A nurse?'

'Not Iris. Heaven help us!' She banged a tray to loosen hardening biscuits. 'Your real mother of course.'

'My—my real mother?' Ann leant against the sink. 'I—I never knew that.'

'Oh lor'!' Brenda Davis stopped what she was doing and gaped at her niece. 'You mean Iris has never told you?'

'No.' Ann shook her head slowly.

'Can't see what harm there is knowing *that.*'

'No.' Ann turned her back to gaze out of the window. So her natural mother had been a nurse. But why had she never been told? Could it possibly have anything to do with her adoptive mother's fears?

THREE

'Do you know *where* she nursed?' Ann asked, struggling to remain calm, to sound normal.

'Why, at the ...' her aunt looked up sharply 'at the—do you know, I don't remember. Somewhere in York I believe.'

'Did ... she come from York, then?'

'Oh, I've no idea,' Aunt Brenda exclaimed dismissively, turning on her mixer and calling above its noise. 'Did your uncle tell you I'd had a letter from Jane?'

'Yes.' Ann turned her hands to the dishes again. 'He said something about the possibility of her coming home.'

'Not right her even considering it. Leaving her husband like that.'

'You mean she's leaving Rick?'

'Well she didn't say so in as many

words, but that's what it seems like.' The noise of the mixer died away.

'Oh dear! That could bring mother hot-foot back from Kenya.'

'*If* she gets to hear about it. I've wired Jane not to tell your parents.'

'Oh but ...'

'Oh I know. Jane'll see her dilemma as another way of getting their undivided attention. No-one'd believe she's five years older than you.'

'I've often wondered—perhaps if I'd been her *real* sister ...?'

'No!' She banged the condiment set on the table. 'She'd still have resented you. Heaven knows how she'd have coped if your mother'd had the six kids she wanted.'

Ann shook her head. 'It was rotten for Mum that she couldn't have any more after Jane. And yet,' she paused and gazed out of the window, 'for me, Mum's misfortune has meant a home I might never have had.'

On her return journey late that afternoon, Ann had much to occupy her mind. She thought back to the conversation with her aunt. The information that her real mother had been a nurse and worked in York, posed all sorts of questions. Should Ann in fact *be* in Hargate to begin her enquiries or would she be better in York?

If Jane did leave her husband and return home, it would be impossible to keep her parents in the dark. Iris would be sure to want to return. Her presence would put a stop to Ann's search, for she'd vowed that her parents would know nothing of it.

She was back in her flat now and was shaken from her reverie by the sound of the telephone.

'Doctor Davis?' enquired a male voice.

'Y-e-s,' she replied haltingly.

'Doctor Ann Davis?'

'That's right.' A slow smile came to her lips as she recognized the voice.

'Iain Kirk. I've been meaning to phone since that night at the airport. When I saw you at the Society Dinner, it jogged my memory.'

'Oh!' Ann was filled with concern. 'Was the damage more than ...'

'No no! Nothing like that.'

'Then why—and how—how did you get *this* phone number?'

'I phoned St Mark's, which was the address you gave me. The operator was most obliging.'

'I see.' But she didn't really. Why was he phoning her now if it wasn't to do with the incident at the airport?

'I had hoped to have a word with you on Friday. Did you leave early?'

'Yes. I ... I had to get back to St Mark's.'

'I've a patient of yours I want to send home.'

'But I don't have any patients yet.'

'One of Arthur Clarke's,' he went on unperturbed. 'Old Arthur doesn't take too kindly to ...'

'Look, Mr Kirk,' Ann felt suddenly,

unreasonably angry, 'I don't take over at the practice until Tuesday. I hardly feel prepared to discuss patients not yet in my care, or, my senior retiring partner!'

'How insensitive of me.' There was a hint of amusement in his voice. 'Until Tuesday then. Meanwhile, do watch out for car headlights.' Now the laughter in his voice was undisguised. 'Folk in Hargate can be a bit touchy. Bye now!'

Ann drew her lips together and glared angrily at the receiver before replacing it in its rest. She was not as angry with Iain Kirk as much as with herself, for rising so readily to Doctor Clarke's defence like that.

By nine o'clock next morning, she'd risen, dressed and breakfasted and was beside her telephone.

'Housing Department,' came the clipped, female voice in reply to Ann's dialling.

'I wonder if you can help me?' she began. 'I'm wanting to trace a family who used to live at number three, Mount Street.'

'Just a minute please.'

Ann could hear background voices and laughter. She waited, her breath short and shallow.

'Not on our records that,' came the reply finally. 'Can't have been Council or we'd have had a record. Private was it?'

'I don't know.'

'Sorry. Can't help you.'

'Just a minute!' Ann was certain the girl was going to ring off. 'Surely *someone* in the town has a record of demolished property?'

'What is it exactly you're wanting?' she asked with exaggerated patience.

'I want to know where the family moved to. The family who used to live at number three, Mount Street.'

'Hold on. I'll put you through to Rates.'

There was a moment's silence, then, ' 'Morning! Rates.'

Again, Ann explained what it was she wanted.

'It's more than six years since that part of Mount Street came down,' the woman told her. 'That's going back a bit.'

'Is there any chance of a forwarding address?' Ann ventured.

'Oh, I doubt it after all this time. Besides, those records'll be down in the basement.'

'It is important. Do you think you might ...?'

'I'll see what I can do. What was the name of the family?'

'Morgan,' Ann heard herself say.

'And the householder's initial?'

'I'm not sure.'

'If you ring back after half an hour, we'll see what we can do.'

That half hour was the longest of Ann's life. At last it was over and the phone in the Rates Office was once more ringing.

'I spoke to you a little earlier about Mount Street ...'

'Oh yes! Now I've an *Annie* Morgan listed, paying rates until July seventy-five when the property came under compulsory purchase.'

Ann held her breath, waiting for more. When the woman didn't go on, Ann prompted. 'And what happened to Mrs Morgan?'

'I've only a care-of address. Sixty, Grange Road.'

'Grange Road, did you say?' Ann's mouth was dry and her heart was racing as she scribbled down the address.

'Yes, but I've checked the Electoral Roll for you and she's not listed at that address now.' The woman's voice was sympathetic.

Ann felt tears of disappointment prick her eyes. 'You've no other records?'

'I'm sorry. You could try the Telephone Directory or there's always Kelly's. The library have copies of Kelly's.'

'Thank you. You've been most helpful.'

There was a whole page of Morgans in the Telephone Directory, but none with A as the initial. Kelly's Directory was now her only hope. That and whoever lived at Sixty, Grange Road. She got out her street map and pored over it until she found the road. First, she'd try the Public Library which was just across the parkland from her flat.

'Kelly's Directory.' The young man in the Reference Library led her to one of the numerous glass cases. 'What year was it you wanted?'

'Nineteen-seventy-five,' she said with assurance, feeling she should start there.

'There you are.' He handed her a well-thumbed volume and returned to his desk.

The streets were listed alphabetically and it took her little time to find Mount Street. Sure enough, against Three, Mount Street, was the name, Annie Morgan. Then she turned to Private Residents list and was able to crosscheck Annie Morgan's name against Mount Street. Her confidence grew in realizing the accuracy of the directory. Seventy-five was the year she was moved out, so the next edition should give her new address and so on up to the present year.

Excitement mounting, she turned to the glass case for the next one in the series. The only ones there were earlier editions. Recent issues must be kept somewhere else.

There were only two other occupants apart from the librarian in the quiet, book-lined room and Ann's footsteps seemed to echo loudly as she crossed to the desk and in a lowered voice, spoke to the young man.

'I'm afraid they stopped publication after the seventy-five edition,' he explained gravely.

'You mean ...?'

'I'm afraid so. Is there some way I might help?'

'I'm trying to trace someone—someone I once knew.'

'There's the Electoral Roll. That's useful for checking against addresses.'

'That's just it. I don't have an address.'

There was a cold wind blowing as Ann made her way back to her flat and all the sunshine seemed to have gone out of the day. She'd just got in and made herself a coffee when the phone rang.

'Arthur Clarke here.'

'Good morning.' Her spirits lifted at hearing his voice.

'I thought you might like to look in today, so's I could show you the ropes on my last day.' He chuckled and Ann felt it was a pity he was retiring for she felt she'd have enjoyed working with him.

When she arrived at the surgery, the patients sitting in the waiting area stared curiously as she passed. The two receptionists were both occupied on different phones and paid little heed as Ann passed them and made her, way through to the office.

'Hi there!' Dr Sean Murdie was just on his way out and almost bowled her over as he swept through the doorway. 'Just had a call-out. See you later.'

Dr John Currie was sitting at a desk going through his mail.

' 'Morning.' He turned and smiled slowly. 'Arthur's through in his room waiting for you.'

The door to Dr Clarke's consulting-room stood open and he was seated at his desk. 'Come in! Come in!' He pressed the bell on his desk. 'I'm taking second surgery.' He indicated a chair by the window. 'Sit in and you'll get to meet some of your patients.'

After the last patient had been seen, Dr Clarke told her how the practice worked and how the work load was divided.

'You'll find you've more time off than when I was a young doctor like you.'

'Won't you miss your patients and this way of life?' Ann asked.

'Of course,' he admitted. 'But I'm looking forward to spending some time with Nancy. I *am* keeping on a few private patients and I'll always be available for locums when I'm needed.'

'Does your wife play golf?' Ann asked, remembering how Nancy had told her of Arthur's plan to play every course in Britain.

'No. But she makes an excellent caddie.' He chuckled, pulling open the drawers of his desk. 'You can leave me now. I'm clearing out.'

She got to her feet. 'Is there anything I can do to help?'

'Thank you, no.' Then as she reached the door. 'There is one last word of advice though. Don't let that fellow, Kirk, have all his own way. If you feel he's sending someone home too early, then tell him as much. They're our patients and we know the home conditions.'

'Right.' Ann nodded, choosing to say nothing about Iain Kirk's phone call the previous evening.

Once outside the surgery building, Ann's mind returned to her search and the only lead remaining. Grange Road was not difficult to find. She pulled up at the opposite side of the road to number sixty and stared at the white-painted board swinging from a tree. 'Grange Nursing Home' was painted in bold, black letters and beneath was a telephone number.

She gazed at the large stone house, from the freshly-painted woodwork to the sparkling, net-curtained windows. So Kathleen Morgan it appeared, had placed Annie Morgan, presumably her mother, into a nursing-home. How long had she been there? Long enough for anyone to remember her?

Ann pondered for a while then drove resolutely away to return to her flat and the anonymity of the telephone.

'The Grange,' came the woman's voice down the line.

'I'm enquiring after a Mrs Annie Morgan.' She tried to alter her voice, to avoid possible recognition in the future.

'Annie Morgan? You've got the wrong number, love. There's no Morgan here.'

'But she *was* there, some years ago.'

'I daresay, love, but no-one stays here forever.'

'Can you ...?' Ann floundered for a moment, 'Can you tell me where she went when she left you?'

'How long since she was here?' A note of exasperation had entered the voice now. 'And who is it calling, anyway?'

'I'm—I'm an old friend.' Ann cleared her throat. 'It was nineteen seventy-five when she came to you.'

'Seventy-five! That's going back a bit. Hang on.'

Ann hung on and hung on until she was sure the woman had gone off duty and someone would come along sooner or later, find the receiver off its rest, replace it and that would be that.

'You still there, love?' came the voice finally.

'Yes. Have you been able ...?'

'She died in December of that year.'

'Oh!'

'Well she was eighty-six, according to this register.'

'Yes of course,' Ann managed feebly.

'Shame you didn't hear,' the woman offered in clumsy sympathy.

'About her relatives. Were there ...?'

'Funny you should ask. Jessie, our cleaner here who remembers everybody, was only just saying how the old lady's granddaughter was a nurse and never let a day pass without visiting her gran.'

Ann clutched at this gem of information. 'This Jessie, would she ... could she ... does she *know* the granddaughter?'

'Ooo, I can't say, I'm sure.'

'You've been so helpful,' Ann gushed. 'Do you think you might just ask her for me?'

'Hang on,' she said with mild forbearance.

Ann tapped nervously on the telephone table, gripping the receiver tightly, straining to catch any background voices.

'Jessie doesn't know her to speak to,'

came the voice down the line, 'but she does know she married soon after her gran died. A councillor, the fellow she married.'

'In Hargate?' Ann prompted.

'Oh yes. She says she still sees her around from time to time.'

'And her married name?'

'She's not sure, except that he's quite a well-known councillor with a name like Dikes or Sikes.' A bell rang persistently in the background. 'Look, I'll have to go now ...'

'Yes of course and thank you, thank you very much.'

'That's all right,' came the cheery reply. 'Anytime!'

Ann sat for some moments, her heart thumping loudly against her chest wall. There must surely be a list of councillors she could ask to see without arousing suspicions. Would they make addresses available too? Then what? Would she be satisfied just to catch a glimpse of her natural mother and where she lived? Or would she want to disclose her identity by writing to request they meet somewhere? The possibilities were endless.

By the time the door closed behind the last patient at evening surgery on Ann's first day, she was feeling completely drained. She leaned back in her chair and looked about her.

The room was the smallest and darkest of the three consulting-rooms but it was her very own and quite adequate for her needs and those of her patients.

All she wanted now was a light supper, a long soak in the bath, soft music on her radio and a comfortable armchair. It was in that precise moment that she remembered James.

Horror of horrors! She'd completely forgotten he was coming for supper. Hastily, she collected up the pile of patients' records and took them through to file away.

The roads were quiet and she made the short journey to her flat in record time. Nevertheless, as she parked her Mini, she caught sight of James sitting in his Cortina at the other side of the road.

'Hello, James,' she called, unable to conceal her weariness.

'Good gracious, Ann, you look all in,' he observed, hurrying to her side.

'Oh, I'm all right,' she shrugged him off. 'Just a little tired.'

As they climbed the stairs towards her flat on the top floor, her telephone was ringing.

'Here! Give me your key,' James demanded. 'I'll dash on and answer that.'

A few moments later, she entered through the flat door just as he was replacing the receiver.

'Wrong number?' she asked.

'No.' He was writing on her telephone pad and didn't look up. 'A chap by the name of Iain Kirk. Phone number's here.'

'What did you tell him?' Ann asked sharply.

'That you were not yet in and would ring him later.' He was scrutinizing the note pad in his hand.

'Well you've no right to have done,' Ann protested.

'It'll be nothing that won't wait until you've had something to eat.'

'How do you know?' she snapped.

'What are these names here?' James asked in a puzzled tone. 'Annie Morgan,' he read from the notepad. 'The Grange? Married councillor ... name of Sikes ... Dikes ...?'

Ann snatched the notepad from him. 'That's private!' she stormed. 'You've no business prying into my affairs!'

It was just as if she had slapped his face. 'Whatever's got into *you?*' he asked with cool surprise. 'Since when have your *affairs,* as you call them, been private from me?'

Something about his tone angered her

further and she turned on her heel. 'If you'll excuse me, I'm tired and I'm going for a bath.'

She knew her reaction was only partly due to tiredness and more to the way James had handled Iain Kirk's phone call. How easily the surgeon would misconstrue their relationship. She didn't stop to ask herself why that should be so important.

And how careless she'd been to let James find that information on her notepad. She didn't want him to know of her discoveries and regretted now ever having confided in him at all. She should have known that this was something she had to do alone.

Ann was suddenly glad that she hadn't pressed her aunt further for more information. It wasn't fair to involve others when there was no way that they could understand her great need. Besides, knowing her adoptive mother's opposition to any contact between Ann and her real mother, it would have placed her aunt in an impossible situation.

Lying soaking in the bath, she knew with increasing certainty that she alone must choose the path ahead. Whether or not to continue with her quest, had to be her decision and hers alone.

FOUR

When Ann finally emerged from her leisurely bath, she dressed slowly, wanting to delay for as long as possible, further inevitable interrogation from James.

Re-entering the living-room however, she found it empty. Surely he'd not ...?

'I'm fixing us an omelette,' came his voice from the small kitchen.

She smiled to herself at this unusual display of domesticity and went to investigate.

James, now in his shirt sleeves, was gently and ineffectually, tapping an egg on the side of one of several cups on the worktop. Two egg boxes and scattered broken shells told their own tale.

'Would you ... would you like me to take over?' she asked cautiously, not stepping beyond the threshold.

'No, no!' The vehemence of his reply had the desired effect on the egg he was trying to crack, whereupon Ann made a hasty retreat, convinced that James would not welcome an onlooker.

'Shout if I can do anything,' she called over her shoulder and went to the telephone and dialled.

'Iain Kirk here.' The voice was immediately recognizable.

'Doctor Davis here. I believe you called a short time ago.

'That's right. Your—er—male secretary would it be ... passed on the message then?'

Male secretary indeed! 'I was told of your call of course.' Ann was fuming, but couldn't suppress a smile at the fellow's impertinence.

A smell of smoking fat came to her from the kitchen and she could hear the sound of the whisk.

'I've put your name forward for an invite

to a symposium in Leeds, in a couple of weeks time.'

'Oh! What symposium is that?' She struggled to shut out the noises from the kitchen and the implications of a burning pan.

'It's mainly of a surgical slant but there's a paper on "Management of post-operative patients at home",' Iain Kirk explained. 'New as you are to general practice, I felt you could find it useful.'

'Well, thank you.' Ann was flustered by his gesture, not sure whether to feel flattered or insulted.

Having glimpsed the adverse reactions to this forward-thinking surgeon, she couldn't help wondering if this was an attempt at getting someone on his side.

'It sounds interesting, but whether I'll be able to attend will depend on my partners of course.'

'You'll have no problems there. They'll be eating out of your hand in no time at all.'

She laughed, then recalling their earlier conversation from Sunday, was prompted to ask, 'Didn't you have a patient to discuss?'

'I *did*. She's gone to stay with her daughter out of town. A letter should be on its way to you.'

'Oh, I see.' She could hear James calling her. 'I must get on now.'

'Look forward to seeing you in Leeds, then.' And with a cheery 'Bye now,' he rang off.

'Ann!' It was James's voice again. 'Didn't you hear me?'

'Coming!'

'Not bad for a first attempt.' He stood back, proudly admiring the half-burnt, leathery-looking omelettes.

'Not bad at all,' Ann agreed later, demolishing the last morsel and getting up to fetch coffee.

'You going to tell me who Annie Morgan is?' James asked on her return.

She went on pouring coffee without

looking up. 'My natural great grand-mother.'

'So you're on the track?' There was no disguising the disapproval in his voice.

'Oh, who knows,' she said dismissively. 'There are hundreds of Morgans in the area.'

She felt his eyes upon her as she stirred her coffee. 'How far do you intend to take this, Ann?'

'Can we please talk about something else?' She got to her feet and went over to her radio and tuned in to a quiet, restful piece of music.

James made no further reference to her quest, but his attitude on the matter overshadowed the remainder of the evening and it was with relief that she finally closed the door on his departing figure.

Life is full of change, she reminded herself after he'd gone. As one door opens another closes. She wondered, not for the first time, how far James would journey through her open door.

Ann gradually began to feel her feet in the practice over the next few days. The routine began to lose its strangeness and between them, her partners offered what assistance they could in trying to smooth the process of her settling in.

She soon learnt that John Currie's reserve was perfectly natural to him and in no way directed only at her. In a completely contrasting style, Sean Murdie's *joie de vivre* often served to glide over awkward moments.

On Friday of that first week, after a heavy morning surgery, Ann was downing a welcome cup of coffee in the office behind reception before starting on an ante-natal clinic.

Joyce, the younger of the two reception-ists, was on the phone and at the same time, flicking through the appointments diary offering a choice of dates to the caller.

'You *can't* see Doctor Davis before Tuesday of next week.'

There was a pause and Joyce raised her eyes heavenwards in exasperation. 'That's right,' she said down the phone with exaggerated patience, 'Doctor Davis *is* the new lady doctor, taken over from Doctor Clarke.'

Another pause.

'Today?' she nearly exploded. 'I'm sorry. She's finished her morning surgery and is about to begin an ante-natal ...'

'What's wrong?' Ann mouthed at the now tight-lipped Joyce

Joyce put a hand over the mouthpiece. 'She's found a lump in her breast and says she can't wait ...'

'Tell her to come along and I'll see her at the end of the ante-natal session,' Ann told her without the slightest hesitation.

'It's not our procedure to book ordinary patients in special clinics,' Joyce reasoned, moments after as she banged down the receiver with appalling bad grace.

'Quite right too,' Ann replied. 'But procedures like rules, are made to be broken when the occasion demands it.'

Ignoring the mumbled retort from the aggrieved receptionist, Ann took the pile of record cards stacked ready for her and went along to her consulting-room.

She entered and moved round the large desk to sit in her chair and reached out to press the bell which would summon the first patient.

'Come in,' Ann called, in reply to a knock on the door. 'Mrs Smart isn't it?' she checked, after glancing at the top record card.

'That's right,' beamed the fresh-faced woman entering and thrusting her heavy abdomen proudly before her.

After the consultation was over, the woman paused before opening the door. 'You've no idea how nice it is to have a lady doctor.'

If Ann was flattered by the woman's compliment, the mixed reception she received from the remainder of the pregnant ladies that Friday morning, soon put her feet back on the ground. Some viewed her with frank suspicion, others with open curiosity and invariably, she felt their eyes travel towards her bare, left-hand ring finger.

She sat for a few moments after the last patient had left the room. Was it possible that twenty-seven years ago, Kathleen Morgan, her mother, might have been examined in this very room? That Doctor Clarke, now retired and then junior partner, should have sat at this very desk as she was doing now?

She planned to call into the Municipal Offices today where a list of councillors was available. It shouldn't be difficult to find a name that sounded like Dikes or Pikes. After that—well, she'd not quite made up her mind. Perhaps ...

A light knocking on the door shook her from her reverie. 'Come in,' she called.

A slight woman in her late forties stood uncertainly on the threshold holding out her record card. 'Mrs Hall,' she managed, in a soft, nervous voice.

Then Ann remembered. 'Of course. Come in, Mrs Hall.'

After a thorough and careful examination, Ann said, 'I'll think we'll have a second opinion.'

'Oh, Doctor!' The woman put a hand to her mouth to stifle a sob.

'Come now, Mrs Hall.' Ann leaned across the desk towards her. 'It doesn't mean it's anything serious. However, if it should be, then Mr Kirk at Hargate General is an expert in this field and will see you get treatment right away.'

'Should I have come sooner, Doctor?' Mrs Hall asked, once she was calm. 'Would it have made any difference?'

'Most things stand a better chance of cure the sooner they are seen and this is especially so with breast lumps.'

'Soon as I knew we had a lady doctor I decided to come. It's not something I could tell a man.'

Ann sighed. What could she say to

that except, 'But they're *doctors,* not just ordinary men.' As soon as she said it she realized how ridiculous it must sound, but at least it had raised a smile on the woman's face.

Iain Kirk's secretary at the General was most cooperative. 'He can see her at his clinic on Monday, Doctor Davis. He always insists we never keep our breast ladies waiting for appointments.'

Mentally, Ann charted up a stroke in his favour. She *would* request time off to attend that symposium. The programme had arrived that very morning and she had it with her so she'd broach the subject now if Doctor Currie was still around.

He was sorting through his mail when she went into the office and took a minute or two to look over the programme she gave him, before replying.

Slowly then, he spun round in his chair. 'How did you come by this?'

'It ... came through the post this morning.' She didn't have to explain *how* she had come to receive it.

'We had notice of it some weeks ago.' He pointed towards the bin for waste paper. 'You must know what Arthur Clarke was like about Kirk and his early discharges.' He waved the programme which listed Iain Kirk as presenting one of the papers. 'Red rag to a bull, this was.'

Ann smiled, remembering the retired doctor's belligerence towards the surgeon.

'Yes.' John Currie handed the programme back. 'You go along. Might pick up some useful tips.' With a slow smile he turned back to his desk.

The Municipal Offices were housed in a gracious old building, fronted by beautiful well-kept flower beds.

Ann entered by the revolving door knowing that if she found the information she was seeking, there would be no turning back. This step would bring her too close for it to be possible to withdraw.

'They're listed in alphabetical order.' The young clerk with heavily made up eyes placed a printed booklet before her on the enquiry desk.

'Thank you.' With thumping heart Ann turned the first page. Armstrong—West Central. Donald—East Central. Mathews —South Edge. Sykes—North Edge. The last name screamed at her from the page. SYKES! That had to be it. A name like Dikes or Pikes. Hastily, she looked down the other names listed. None held any remote resemblance.

Sykes, Henry, 2 Park Close, Hargate. That had to be him. Park Close! She'd actually been there to see a patient yesterday—an elderly man recovering from a stroke. She remembered thinking what a pleasant road it was—a quiet cul-de-sac, adjacent to a large park. To think how near she had been. But this of course was the danger in a town this small.

After a final and lingering scrutiny, she closed the booklet. 'Thanks,' she called over to the young clerk and made her way out of the building.

Like the pieces of a jigsaw puzzle, she began to fit together what she now knew of her natural mother. Kathleen Morgan had worked at some time as a nurse in York, but in nineteen fifty-five, while with child, had resided at 3 Mount Street with her grandmother, Annie Morgan. There was a gap then until nineteen seventy-five when her grandmother moved to The Grange. There, Kathleen visited her daily until the old lady died in December of that year. Shortly after, Kathleen married a Henry Sykes and was now living at 2 Park Close.

The impulse to drive immediately to look at the house, perhaps even to catch a glimpse of her mother, had to be abandoned in the knowledge that her car could now be recognized. It only needed her old gentleman patient to be looking out which would lead to all sorts of questions. He was on her list for weekly visits so she'd just have to be patient.

Ann was week-end call doctor and

on Sunday, after a busy morning with numerous calls, she had just finished lunch when the phone rang.

'Oh, Doctor, can you come?' It was a woman's voice, full of agitation. 'It's my father. He's taken a turn for the worse.'

'And your father's name?' Ann prompted.

'Mr Wood.'

'Mr Wood,' Ann repeated carefully. 'And the address?'

'Park Close, Doctor. I always visit Sundays and I can't wake him.'

'Park Close. Number ...?'

'Seven, Doctor. Oh dear, what'll I do?'

'Just stay calm. I'll be right there.'

'Stay calm' Ann had told the woman and now repeated the words to herself over and over, until averting her eyes from any other house in the close, she pulled up outside the open door of number seven.

'He's in here, Doctor.' The well-dressed woman who'd been looking out for her, led her into the front room where Mr Wood had his bed.

It didn't take Ann long to establish that her patient, who she had seen only a few days previously, had suffered another stroke.

'I'm afraid it'll mean hospital, Mrs ...?'

'*Miss*, Doctor. Miss Wood. I am his daughter though I don't live here. That's why ...' her voice faltered.

Ann crossed to the telephone. 'If you'll just excuse me ...'

While they waited for the ambulance, Miss Wood gathered together a few of her father's toilet requisites.

'Where do you live?' Ann asked.

'Across in Lancashire,' the woman said gravely. 'I'm a teacher.'

'I see.'

'I wanted him to come to me last year,' she hurried on, 'after the stroke, but he wouldn't hear of it.'

'Is this his home town?'

'Oh yes. Never lived anywhere else.'

'Then you can understand him not wanting to move ...'

'Oh yes!'

'He was telling me, during the week, how marvellous his neighbours are.'

'Yes. Though I hardly know them. I sometimes thinks he cares more for them than he does for me.'

The ambulance arrived just then making further conversation impossible.

Once having seen her patient safely aboard, with his daughter intending to follow by car, Ann prepared to leave. She was at the front door when the click of the garden gate heralded the arrival of a neighbour.

She guessed she was a neighbour because of the carpet slippers she wore, which, like the woollen dress covering her spare frame, appeared as if a size too large for her.

'I saw the ambulance,' she said in a soft voice. 'Mr Wood, is he ...?' Her lined, too-thin face was full of concern as she came nearer to Ann.

'My father's had another stroke,' Miss Wood informed her coldly from the doorway.

'Oh, I am sorry.' The woman inclined her head to one side in genuine sympathy and clasped her hands together. 'Perhaps I should have looked in this morning, but he was fine yesterday when I brought him a drop of home-made soup ...' Her voice, as if suddenly embarrassed, faded off.

'That was kind,' Ann began, stepping into the path.

'Oh it was nothing. Nothing at all.' She turned to Miss Wood. 'Is—is there anything at all I can do to help?'

'Well I ...' Miss Wood opened her hands in an awkward gesture, 'I ... I don't really know yet.'

'Well, I'm Kathleen Sykes from across the way at number two,' the softly spoken woman went on kindly. 'If you think of anything, just call on me.' She turned then and walked back down the garden path.

Ann looked after her, her heart racing

and pounding like a run-away express train. She willed herself to remain calm.

'There goes my mother' a voice inside her was saying 'my mother, my mother, my ...' until she had to bite her lips together tightly for fear of shouting out the words.

She didn't know how long she stood there, looking after her as she crossed the road and made her way through the gate and up the garden path, finally disappearing into the house opposite.

Ann never knew how she reached the sanctity of her car, but reach it she did, somehow.

This wasn't the way she'd imagined things would be. She'd thought of it in the terms of a reunion—a mother and her long lost child. She'd planned a preliminary letter or phone call. Not this way. Perhaps James *had* been right. Perhaps she should have left well alone.

A surreptitious glance at the house across the road gave Ann a glimpse of bright orange curtains, and window boxes with clusters of cheerful daffodils and early-flowering tulips.

If she could be sure that Kathleen Sykes was alone in that house, she could go over there now and reveal her true identity.

Supposing she wasn't alone? Supposing her husband was there? What if there were children? What if none of them, but her mother knew of her existence?

With such thoughts filling her head, Ann switched on the ignition and drove away.

While she drove, she tried to conjure up the image of her mother and found no difficulty. She saw clearly the greying hair which fell in soft curls to frame the too-thin, lined face. She heard again the softly spoken voice reaching out with offers of help to Mr Wood's daughter. But more than all that, she saw the loose-fitting dress on the spare frame and the too-big carpet slippers and shuddered involuntarily in the fear that her mother, now she'd found her, was far from being a fit woman.

Yet what could there possibly be, about that gentle woman, that could cause her adoptive mother to feel threatened? What had made Iris Davis so fearful of any contact?

FIVE

On return to her flat, Ann sat by the window looking out over the wide expanse of grassland. Dark clouds were gathering, threatening rain, which only served to accentuate her melancholy.

She thought of her parents out in Kenya and of her sister, Jane, and husband, Rick, out in Bermuda. She thought of her aunt and uncle on the farm, and of James and the recent quarrels between them. She thought of her patients, young and old, yet all the while her mind kept returning to Park Close and Kathleen Sykes.

All the anticipated joy in finding her, was strangely overshadowed by the predicament she now found herself in.

She was relieved when the phone rang shaking her from her reverie.

'Nancy Clarke here!'

'Oh! Hello!'

'Arthur and I wondered if you would come over and join us for an evening meal? That's if you're not doing anything already?'

'I'd love to,' Ann warmed at the thought of seeing the retired doctor and his wife again, 'but I'm afraid I'm on call.'

'Oh!' Disappointment hung heavy in her voice. 'Just a minute, dear. What's that, Arthur?'

There followed a few exchanged remarks in the background, then, 'Arthur says, could we come over to you?'

'Yes of course.' Ann's mind immediately leapt ahead to what she could give them to eat. But she hadn't allowed for Nancy Clarke's thoughtfulness.

'That's settled then. We'll bring supper with us, so no need for you to do a thing.'

After a tour of the flat the doctor's wife guided Ann towards the settee. 'Just sit down there and talk to Arthur will you, while I take over your kitchen.'

'Oh no, I ...'

'You'll be doing me a favour, dear,' the older woman argued. 'This man of mine,' she linked an arm fondly through her husband's, 'is missing his patients something awful and you can begin by reassuring him that they're all managing very well without him.'

'Don't believe a word of it.' Arthur Clarke chuckled. 'Never given any of them a thought since I left. Nevertheless,' he sat down and patted the place beside him, 'no harm in telling me what you've been up to.'

So Ann told him, not everything of course, but of those patients who she knew he felt particular concern.

'And today,' he prompted, 'anything serious to cope with?'

'Mr Wood's had another stroke, I'm afraid.'

'Well I'll be ...' He banged his thigh

with the flat of his hand. 'His daughter would be there with it being Sunday, was she?'

'She was.' Ann went on to explain how things were, not trusting herself to mention the call from Kathleen Morgan.

'He's his neighbours to thank for ever getting home after his last stroke,' Arthur told her. 'Marvellous ...'

'Come and get it!' Nancy's voice from the kitchen put a stop to their conversation so that Ann felt let down for she thought he might be going to tell her something relevant.

Several times during the salad meal, she tried to summon the courage to incline Arthur towards their interrupted discussion, but on each occasion she shied from the final step.

It was while she was clearing away that she heard him say to his wife. 'Ann tells me old Charlie Wood's had another stroke.'

'Poor old Charlie.'

'You started to tell me about his

neighbours,' Ann rushed in, struggling to sound normal.

'I was only going to say how they've washed him, fed him, shopped for him ...'

'As if one of them hadn't enough on her plate,' the doctor's wife interrupted.

'You mean Katie of course,' Arthur Clarke said.

Ann held her breath.

'All her life she's slaved for others, in one way or another,' the doctor went on. 'You know Henry's in hospital again?'

'Huh!' Nancy grunted. 'She must be the best thing that ever came his way.' She then turned to Ann who had been endeavouring to appear only mildly interested. 'If you've not already heard of our Councillor Sykes, you soon will.'

Her husband chuckled. 'He's not that bad, Nancy. Hargate needs outspoken citizens like Henry.'

'Outspoken maybe. Unpleasant, no.'

'Ah well! Maybe that good woman'll ...'

'Not a chance. Once a tiger, always a

tiger.' Nancy stretched her legs out, feet together, thoughtfully. 'She deserves the George Medal for taking him on.'

'Mmm. But it cuts both ways.' Arthur took his pipe from his inside pocket. 'Not many men of his age would take on a woman with two kids.'

Nancy only snorted, while Ann waited with baited breath for him to go on.

'You shouldn't come across him too often,' Arthur told Ann. 'He's one of the handful of private patients I told you I was keeping on.' He tapped the cup of his pipe into the palm of his hand. 'Mind if I smoke?'

Ann smiled her assent, passing him an ashtray. Hungry though she was for more information about her mother, she dare not risk arousing suspicion by asking questions.

After they left, she lay awake long into that night going over and over the day's events.

Kathleen Sykes's two children, presumably by an earlier marriage, would be *her* half brothers or sisters. That was something she had made no allowance for. What of her previous marriage? Had she been a widow or divorcee when she'd married this seemingly unpleasant man, Sykes?

How dearly Ann would have loved to know more, perhaps even to have confided in Arthur and Nancy Clarke now that she'd abandoned James as her only confidant. She felt the older couple would have been able to view the situation objectively and advise her on where to go from here. Yet to speak to them of it, may be to jeopardize her mother's good name, to two folk who obviously held her in high regard.

Instead, she threw herself into her work, often not stopping for lunch breaks and frequently taking on extra duties from her two colleagues. Yet however busy she was, constantly lurking in her mind was the desire to contact her mother. She even got as far as trying to write a letter, but after several attempts had to abandon the idea, at least for the time being.

The evening before the symposium, Ann had just sat down to write to her parents in Kenya, when the phone rang.

'Ah! No male secretary on hand tonight?'

'I don't have a secretary,' Ann pointed out. 'Male or female.'

'I'm pleased to hear that,' Iain Kirk remarked. 'Now then. About tomorrow.'

'Yes?'

'With petrol so costly and the threat to headlights, I wondered if you'd care to give your car a day off and come in mine?'

'Oh but ...'

'Right! That's settled. Oak Grove, number twenty, isn't it?'

'Yes, that's right, but however did you ...?'

He chuckled. 'It's not difficult in a small town like Hargate. Can you be ready for eight-thirty?'

'Yes. Yes of course.'

After he'd rung off, Ann felt a strange stir of excitement and told herself it was only because Iain Kirk was so different to James. He was everything that James was not and she had to admit he was more than a refreshing change.

She awoke to a cold, grey morning, but the weather did little to dampen her spirits as she dressed hurriedly in a cheery red woollen suit, which she avoided for work as being a little garish, but always felt good in.

She was at the window when the blue TR7 pulled up outside and she instantly recognized the tall, dark man clambering out.

'A TR Seven,' she said to herself dreamily. 'That's why he wanted to take me. Who wouldn't want to show off a model like that?'

He must have spotted her just then for he waved up and grinned. She lifted a hand in greeting and went quickly down to meet him.

'My!' he greeted her appraisingly, 'no fear of a dull day with you around.'

Even as he said it, the heavens opened and it began to rain so that they had to scramble for the cover of the car.

'Well! How do you like her?' Iain asked, once they were out on the open road.

'She's beautiful,' Ann enthused, as the car sped along like some sleek and silent creature of the jungle.

'The old one was never quite the same after someone hit her headlight one night.'

'Ohh!' Ann protested. 'Will you never let me forget that?'

'Of course I will,' he replied without conviction. 'But tell me first, what were you doing out there that night?'

So she told him about her parents' departure for East Africa.

'Must have been a painful parting. Couldn't your male secretary have gone with you to ease the ...?'

Ann groaned. 'Won't you leave that alone. As a matter of fact, I chose to go alone.'

'I see,' he murmured, sensing her mood.

'And what were you doing at the airport?'

'Meeting a friend who doesn't believe in taxis while mugs like me will play chauffeur.'

'Wise friend I would say, especially now the vehicle's a TR7.' She couldn't help wondering if it had been male or female as she looked out at the driving rain. A comfortable silence settled over them while the windscreen wipers swept back and forth, back and forth.

At length, Iain said. 'Your breast-lump lady was in theatre yesterday.'

'And?' Ann turned to look at him, anxious to hear the outcome.

'Benign,' he said with satisfaction.

'Thank God for that. Just think of the months of worry she could have saved herself.'

'Happens all too often,' he agreed, then put out an arm and switched on the car radio.

On arrival at the new modern hospital,

they were directed to the Post Graduate Centre where, after signing in, Iain rested a hand on her shoulder. 'I'll have to leave you, but we'll meet up for lunch.' Then he was gone and she saw he was taking his place with the panel of speakers up on the platform.

It was an interesting and absorbing morning so that Ann was surprised when it was suddenly lunch-time.

Iain was obviously well known to many present and though they managed two seats to enjoy their buffet lunch, he was constantly approached by other delegates, so that there was little opportunity for more than a brief exchange of words together.

During the afternoon session, his own paper was skilfully and professionally presented, and though dissension was apparent, he handled any questions with such adroitness, that few were not in agreement with him by the end of the day.

'Well!' he asked on the way home, 'did you enjoy it?'

'Immensely!' she replied honestly and wanted to add 'every minute since you collected me this morning' but thought better of it. It's the excitement of a TR7, she told herself, reluctantly climbing out when he pulled up outside her flat.

Iain was already out, holding open the gate. 'I'm sorry I can't come in for a drink, but I've a ward round to do—so perhaps some other time?'

Ann couldn't stop from laughing. 'I never even asked you,' she protested.

'Oh, but I knew you were going to.' His face lit up in a smile. 'I sensed you were just waiting for the right moment.'

'Oh!' She waltzed through the open gate. 'Has no-one ever told you, you are quite impossible!'

'Many's the time,' he called after her. 'Bye now. Be seeing you.'

'Bye,' she condescended, 'and thanks for the lift.' She stood on the steps of the old house and watched as he drove off.

It must have been after nine o'clock that evening, when unexpectedly, the phone rang.

'Doctor Davis?' came a deep masculine voice.

'Yes.'

'Doctor Cameron here from Hargate General. Your patient, Mr Sykes, was discharged this afternoon. I want ...'

'Mr—Sykes—?' Ann became flustered. There must be some mistake.

'Councillor Sykes,' he said in a tone that was obviously intended to disperse any remaining doubt. 'Old Arthur's off golfing in Scotland and your receptionist tells me you're looking after his patients in his absence.'

Instant denial leapt to her lips but died there despite the waves of fear, of apprehension, washing over her. 'I—I see.' Then she had to struggle to give her full attention while he detailed one or two problems which would require firm and careful supervision.

'Perhaps I better warn you,' he finished, with a hint of laughter in his voice, 'he's not too fond of women attending him.'

'Thank you, Doctor Cameron. I'm sure I shall manage.'

All night she tossed and turned searching for some feasible excuse that she might offer one of her colleagues, to take on Mr Sykes. Finally, she knew there was simply no way out of her dilemma and she reminded herself that surely this was the kind of opportunity she wanted. Here was a chance to see her mother in her own home, perhaps even the chance to find out why she looked so poorly.

It was just past noon the following day as Ann turned into Park Close. Her heart thumped loudly against her chest wall, as with eyes down, she made her way up the garden path of number two.

Kathleen Sykes, as she'd introduced herself that day over at old Mr Wood's, opened the door.

'I'm Doctor Davis,' Ann managed, in a voice she hardly recognized as her own.

The woman nodded politely and led her silently across the hall. In the fleeting seconds before she'd turned away, Ann had taken in the drawn, strained features. Something in her moved her to speak out.

'Mrs Sykes,' she whispered, halting the woman in her tracks.

'What is it, Doctor?' She only half turned and kept her eyes averted.

'Are you ...? Do you ...?' But she couldn't get the words out. 'How—how's he been since he came home?'

'Much the same,' she replied in a flat voice, giving nothing away, edging to lead upstairs.

An outburst of noisy young voices raised in disagreement, came from a downstairs room.

Mrs Sykes turned, mumbled something which sounded like 'Mother of Mercy' and pushed open the door from where the voices came. 'Did I not specially ask you to be quiet?' she pleaded in her soft voice. 'He's still very sick up there and the doctor's here just now.'

There were murmurings of 'Sorry, Mum' amidst nervous giggles before Mrs Sykes re-emerged, pulling the door to behind her.

'Who's that?' a voice bellowed as they reached the top of the stairs and crossed the landing.

'It's just the doctor,' the woman called softly, opening a door and showing her visitor in.

'About time too,' the man grunted from his bed. He looked about sixty with a brick-red face and bushy eyebrows. His shoulders were rounded so that his near bald head had a forward belligerent thrust. 'This how you treat all your patients?'

Ann smiled, her professional training coming to the rescue. 'I'm sorry, Mr Sykes, had you expected me sooner?'

'It's *Councillor* Sykes, and yes, I did expect you before now.' He waved an arm at the woman hovering in the open doorway. 'Off with you, Kate, while the *doctor,*' here his voice was thick with derision, 'examines me.'

'Is Kate—your ...?' Ann began after the door closed, still hoping there may be some mistake.

'My wife!' he grunted from his bent position while the young doctor sounded the back of his chest. 'Can't see her lasting as long as my first, mind you.'

'Oh?' Ann slipped her stethoscope into her jacket pocket.

'Too nice by half. And too many hangers-on. Well?' He lay back against his pillows. 'What have you to say for yourself? How do you find me?'

'As well as I expected,' she said guardedly.

'You've never seen me before.' He glowered at her beneath bushy eyebrows. 'How could you know what to expect?'

'Doctor Cameron had a few words with me ...'

'Did he, by Jove! How much did he tell you?' Again the forward thrust of his head as he fixed her with a hostile glare.

But Ann wasn't to be drawn in this way. 'He told me nothing you don't know yourself,' she said carefully.

'Huh! Thinks I was born yesterday and can't stomach the truth, that's what.'

'You're wrong, Mr Sykes ...'

'Councillor Sykes! And I'm never wrong.'

Ignoring the correction, Ann went on, 'Have you been downstairs yet today?'

'Downstairs?' he bellowed. 'How can a sick man get downstairs?'

'Henry! Henry!' Mrs Sykes re-entered the room. 'Don't you remember old Doctor Clarke telling you how important it was not to get over-excited?'

'All right. All right.' Then he fixed Ann with half closed eyes. 'If getting up and going downstairs kills me—on your head be it!' He slid down the bed then turned on his side. 'Get her out of here will you, Kate?'

'I'm just leaving, *Councillor* Sykes,' Ann said pointedly. 'I'll look in in a week's time. Meanwhile, you know how to reach me, Mrs Sykes?'

'Yes thank you, Doctor.' She nodded gravely, standing by her husband's bed, one hand on his shoulder.

Such was the image of her mother that Ann took away with her as she let herself out of the house. Why oh why, she asked herself, had she not had the courage to ask one of her colleagues to take on this case?

SIX

Over the next few days, Ann fully expected a summons from Councillor Sykes. When in fact it came, it was quite different from what she'd expected.

'It's Sykes here,' rapped the harsh voice in her ear as soon as she picked up the receiver. 'You'd better get here pretty smartish.'

'What is it?' Ann's heart began to race as she swung her feet to the floor and saw from her alarm clock it was two a.m.

'It's Kate.' There was bewilderment in his gruff voice. 'She's ... well she seems to be in some kind of—of collapse.'

'Just stay with her. I'll be there right away.'

The streets were deserted and Ann found

herself willing her little car on, urging it to go ever faster.

After what seemed an eternity, she turned into Park Close and pulled up outside the only house where a light was showing. Even as she went through the gate, the front door opened revealing Mr Sykes in pyjamas and dressing-gown silhouetted against the lighted hall. 'That you, Doctor?' There was a note of urgency in his voice.

For answer, Ann hurried the last few steps and went quickly over the threshold into the house. 'What happened?' she pressed. 'Where is she?'

'She's in here.' Ignoring her first question he led her across the hall into what was presumably the lounge, where Kate Sykes lay prostrate on the settee.

Her face was ashen and beads of perspiration stood out on her forehead. Her eyes were closed, her lips pallid, her breath coming in rapid, shallow gasps.

'Mrs Sykes!' Ann's heart pounded within

her as she watched for some response.

The head moved and the eyes half opened. Then Kate's lips parted and with her tongue she tried to moisten her dry lips.

'It's Doctor Davis.' Ann knelt on the floor beside her mother and as she did so, moved aside a bowl containing vomit.

'Kept nothing down since last night,' Mr Sykes said.

Resting her fingers on the thin wrist, Ann felt the racing pulse. 'Mrs Sykes!' she urged, and this time was rewarded by an attempt at a smile.

'Oh Doctor,' came the faint whisper. 'So sorry—so sorry to bring you out like this.'

Ann swallowed the lump in her throat, willing her nerves to be steady, to treat this situation objectively as if before her, was just another of her many patients. 'Now I want you to try and answer a few simple questions for me.' She turned to Mr Sykes, hovering at her elbow. 'I'd love a cup of tea or coffee in a little while, if you could manage it.'

Without answering, he left the room enabling Ann to proceed with her examination.

It took her little time to reach her diagnosis and she studied Mrs Sykes's lined face before telling her gently. 'You're going to have to go into hospital.'

'Oh no, Doctor!' A hand gripped Ann's arm and alarm showed in the dark eyes. 'Henry's not well. He couldn't manage the boys and everything.'

'Mrs Sykes,' Ann began firmly, 'your husband is quite well enough. How old are the boys?'

'Eleven and twelve, Doctor, but ...' she grimaced with pain and struggling to sit up, retched violently.

When she'd settled again, Ann said, 'Where are the boys just now?'

'Oh they're sleeping, Doctor.'

'Right. So just now it's *you* we've got to worry about.'

The door opened and Mr Sykes re-entered Ann got to her feet. 'If I could just use your phone. I'm going to arrange for your wife to go into hospital.'

'What! In the middle of the night? Can't *you* do something?'

'No.' She lowered her voice. 'She must go into hospital.'

'Henry ...' Mrs Sykes urged. 'What about the boys?'

'We'll work something out,' he mumbled. 'Best do as the doctor says.'

'I'm afraid he's in theatre,' the hospital operator told Ann when she asked for the house surgeon on call. 'Can I take a message?'

'Not really.' She paused only briefly. 'Can you get me his boss, Mr Kirk?'

'He's in theatre too.'

'Would you see if one of them could come to the phone?'

She hadn't long to wait. 'Iain Kirk here.'

'Mr Kirk. Doctor Davis here. I ...'

'Ann! What are you doing up at this hour?'

'Working. Same as you.' Then on a serious note. 'I've an acute obstruction. Can you take her?'

'Of course. Tell me a little bit about her.'

Ann told him.

'Doesn't sound too good. I could come out and see her,' he offered. 'But I think better to get her in smartish.'

The ambulance wasn't long in coming and as the two men were transferring their patient onto a stretcher, a frightened young voice from the doorway surprised everyone in the room.

'What you doing with my mum?'

Ann looked at Mr Sykes, willing him to go to the boy, but he only eyed him awkwardly from beneath bushy eyebrows.

'It's all right,' Ann comforted. 'Something's gone wrong with your Mum's insides, so we're taking her to hospital to get it put right.'

'Ben!' his mother called weakly.

'Mum!' The boy moved to her side and clasped the hand she put out.

'I'll ... I'll be back ... soon as possible,' she managed.

'Meanwhile ...' she raised a hand to his cheek, 'you and Paul ... do what you can to help ...' her voice tailed off.

'Have to be getting along, sonny.' One of the ambulance men made clear his intentions by gently taking Mrs Sykes's arms and tucking them inside the blanket covering her.

'I'll see about getting you some help tomorrow,' Ann told Mr Sykes as she left to follow the ambulance in her own car.

Casualty had been alerted, presumably by Iain Kirk and a green-uniformed sister was there to meet them.

'She's to go straight to X-ray then along to female surgery where Mr Kirk will see her,' she told Ann dismissively.

'I could go with her,' Ann volunteered, 'as she's no-one with her.'

'Oh there's no need for that, Doctor. My nurse will accompany her.'

So Ann stood there, helplessly watching, while her mother was wheeled away from her down the stark, hospital corridor.

Sister was only doing what she would with any patient, she told herself. How could she know the woman on the stretcher was no ordinary woman?

The hospital was cloaked in an eerie silence and Ann's footsteps echoed loudly as she made her way across the hall and out through the heavy, swing doors.

Sleep wouldn't come to her again and at seven-thirty prompt, she phoned through to Night Sister at Hargate General.

'Well she's been to theatre,' Sister told her, 'but she's still very poorly.'

'Do you know what the findings were?'

'You'd need to have a word with Mr Kirk about that.'

'Yes of course.'

After replacing the receiver, Ann tapped her fingers nervously on the telephone table. Should she phone Iain Kirk or would he be snatching a few hours sleep? Perhaps she'd wait another half-hour or so.

After showering, she dressed and made herself some coffee and toast. She was deep in thought when the phone rang.

'You awake yet?'

She sighed with relief at the sound of his voice. 'Of course I am.'

'Look, it's about this woman you sent in last night. How well do you know her?'

Ann's knees went weak. 'How ... well ... how do you mean?' Surely he couldn't suspect ...

'The set-up with her husband. Home conditions and all that.'

'You're not ... you're not thinking of sending her home?' Ann floundered, bewildered by his questions.

'No way!' he assured her.

'What is it then?'

'Look! I'm on my way to the hospital now. I'd rather not discuss this over the telephone. Can I call round?'

Ann's hands shook. What had he to tell her that he couldn't discuss on the phone? She'd surely not said anything which could possibly lead him to think there was any connection between her and Kathleen Sykes.

She opened the flat door and left it ajar to save him ringing. He wasn't long in arriving. 'Hi there!' came his familiar voice.

'Hello.' She put her head round the kitchen door. 'Sit down and I'll fetch you a coffee.'

'I'd rather have it through here,' he said, coming into the kitchen and perching on one of her two high stools.

'Okay.' She smiled at him, her insides churning.

'The long and short of it is,' Iain began, 'I had a talk with your Mrs Sykes before taking her to theatre. She suspected the worst and begged me to be honest with her about what I found, but in no way was her husband to be told.'

'And ...?'

'It's as I feared.' He looked up and met her gaze. 'She has cancer.'

An icy hand settled over the place where Ann's heart had been. She closed her eyes, struggling for the right words to say. 'I see.' She heard her voice as if far away. 'How ... how bad?'

'Hey. Come on.' Iain reached out and put a hand on her arm. 'You'd think you'd seen a ghost. If you take all your patients as seriously as this, you'll soon go under.'

'I'm sorry.' How could he know the effect of what he'd just told her? 'It's just ... well, I get the impression she's enough on her plate without this.'

'It's often the way. But you asked how bad. I'd say pretty bad, but not without hope.'

Ann nodded but remained silent. He still hadn't explained why he was here.

'She's going to need further surgery of course. I only relieved the obstruction last night—she was too shocked for anything more.'

'So what are you going to tell her?'

'The truth, or as much as I feel she can take. It's not that which troubles me.'

'What is it then?' Ann pressed.

'How much to tell her husband. Councillor Sykes is not a man to cross. I don't want ...'

'But if she specially asked you not to tell him ...'

'And as their family G.P. you'd go along with that?'

'I'm not their family G.P. They're Doctor Clarke's patients.'

'But I thought he'd retired.'

Ann explained, concluding, 'And he's not due back for a few weeks.'

'Huh! Fine time to choose to go away. And in his absence? Do we fall in with the patient's wishes?'

'Yes,' she replied unhaltingly. 'As far as we possibly can.'

'Very well.' He glanced at his watch. 'My morning's list starts in ten minutes.' He got to his feet and grinned. 'I'll be in touch. Thanks for the coffee.'

Ann saw him out, then crossed to the window and watched as he hurried down the path and out through the gate to his waiting car. Whatever her mother's chances, she knew that at least she was in the hands of a very competent and caring man.

She was already behind schedule now and would be late for morning surgery, but felt she must phone the Sykes's home.

'Paul Sykes here,' came the tremulous young voice. 'Who's speaking please?'

'It's Doctor Davis. I ...'

'I'll take that,' came Mr Sykes's voice, cutting through her words. 'You get off to school.' Then into the mouthpiece. 'Hello. Who's that?'

'Doctor Davis.'

'Oh yes. Well I've just been onto the hospital and they tell me she's had her operation and's as well as can be expected.'

'That's right. Now I'm going to try and get you a Home Help so ...'

'No need,' he came back sharply. 'I've phoned her mother in York and she's coming over. Couldn't stand her for long, but I hear this fellow, Kirk, sends his patients home as soon as possible.'

'Yes but ...'

'Don't bother. Besides, Doctor Clarke's our real doctor, though I appreciate you coming out like that last night.'

'Well, Doctor Clarke's still away so I'll be looking in on you, probably tomorrow.'

It was only when Ann arrived home early evening that she remembered James was coming for dinner. Her friend, June, was coming too with fiancé, Pete.

Struggling to push to the back of her mind all thoughts of the Sykes, she tried to give her mind over to the meal she had already half planned.

James was first to arrive and brought with him a bottle of wine and a bunch of flowers. Placing them on the hall table, he took hold of both her hands and searched her face. 'I've missed you,' he told her. 'Terribly.'

She laughed lightly. 'Oh, I've been so busy.'

'I can see that.' He held onto her hands with a firmer grip. 'You've got shadows under your eyes.'

'Have I?' she laughed again and freeing her hands, picked up the flowers and sniffed them. 'They're lovely.' She turned to go. 'I'll just put them in some water.'

'Not so fast.' He put a restraining hand on her arm. 'Come and sit down first and tell me what you've been doing.'

While she was telling him, June and Pete arrived and within minutes, their infectious mood of frivolity had rubbed off on Ann, totally relaxing her, so that even the dark cloud of anxiety over Kathleen Sykes was temporarily lifted.

They examined her flat amid whoops of admiration declaring that if they could find anything half as nice, they'd get married immediately.

'But I thought it was a buyers market?' James cut in.

'To be perfectly honest,' Pete confided, 'we've found a place we both love, but there's the problem of a sitting tenant.'

Several topics were discussed between the four friends over dinner and the relaxed atmosphere continued until Pete brought up the subject of the recent symposium in Leeds. 'I didn't attend, but another chap in the practice went along. Claims this fellow, Kirk, had every delegate eating out of the palm of his hand before he was finished.'

Ann couldn't suppress her laughter at the memory. 'A slight exaggeration, I'd say.'

'You were there were you?' Pete raised his eyebrows.

'Yes. It was very interesting.'

'Of course! Kirk's a surgeon here in Hargate,' Pete remembered. 'You must have come across him, Ann?'

'Oh yes. I've met him.'

'Kirk?' James frowned. 'Wasn't he the fellow who phoned here one night? Didn't I write his name down and tell him you'd call him back?'

'It may have been,' Ann replied.

'You didn't say you'd been to Leeds, Ann,' James challenged her.

'Didn't I? There was so much to tell you I ...'

'How long did it take you, Ann?' Pete wanted to know. 'Here to Leeds?'

'About twenty minutes, I suppose.'

'You can add at least ten minutes to that,' James intervened. 'Ann invariably drives too fast.'

'James! That's not so. I never exceed the speed limit. As a matter of fact,' she added, rising to clear the main course, 'I wasn't driving on that occasion.'

'Oh!' Pete teased good-naturedly. 'And who was?'

'Iain Kirk gave me a lift,' she told him, deliberately clashing the cutlery.

'Did he, by Jove!' Pete laughed, while James retained a stony silence.

The matter was then dropped and though James eventually broke his silence, he remained very cool for the rest of the evening. It wasn't the first time Ann had been made aware of his possessive nature but she'd long since vowed, it was a side of him she wouldn't give way to.

Her sleep that night was disturbed, not by James's mood but by thoughts of the woman, who twenty-six years ago, had given birth to her and now lay in a hospital bed with cancer, and with no-one it seemed to share the burden. It didn't seem right that as her daughter, Ann couldn't go to her with flowers or just words of comfort, to let her know she cared.

When she called at the Sykes's home next day, the door was opened by an elderly woman of very generous proportions, who despite that, held a striking resemblance to Kathleen Sykes.

'You must be the young doctor my son-in-law's told me about?'

'That's right.' Ann stepped into the hall.

'I'm Mrs Morgan,' she said importantly. 'Kathleen's mother. Young fool, neglecting herself and causing all this bother.'

'Neglecting herself? Now whoever ...?'

'My son-in-law, Doctor.' She dropped her voice to a confidential tone. 'He says how she's been running around after other folk and disregarding her own health.' She thrust out her heavy bosom. 'Not that that's new.'

Ann counted to ten. For the first time, the thought struck her that this woman before her, with her misguided judgement, was her grandmother by birth.

'I do know how very good she's been to one of her elderly neighbours, Mrs Morgan,' Ann said with measured patience. 'As for disregarding her own health, I ...'

'Oh, I could tell you a thing or two,' the elderly woman interrupted.

'Maybe, but I called here to see Mr Sykes,' Ann reminded her, looking towards the stairs.

'Oh, he's up and dressed and working in his study.' She pointed to a door off the hall. 'And he does like to be called *Councillor.*'

The door in question was thrust open just then. 'Can't a fellow work in peace without ... oh, it's you, Doctor!'

'Oh dear!' Mrs Morgan tutted. 'Have we disturbed you?'

Totally ignoring her, Henry Sykes turned to Ann. 'Come in here will you, Doctor?'

Once the door was closed, he turned to Ann. 'Nothing but a pest, that woman. The sooner Kate's back ...'

'How is she this morning?'

'Fairly comfortable, whatever that means in hospital jargon.' He dug his hands deep into his trouser pockets. 'I'm going in today to see for myself.'

'You sure you're well enough?'

'Course I am,' he said shrugging off her

remark. 'Damn sight better than Kate is just now, anyways.'

Ann warmed to the man for the first time and wondered how much of his aggressiveness was merely a front.

After a brief examination, she left quietly through the front door, relieved not to have to cross paths again with Mrs Morgan. But she hadn't allowed for the woman's persistence. Ann had reached the bottom of the path when she heard the steps behind her.

'Here, Doctor. I'd like to know what's wrong with Kathleen and how ...?'

'Oh I really couldn't say,' Ann was quick to reply. 'You'd need to have a word with Mr Sykes. After all, he is her next of kin and ...'

'Funny one that!' she snorted. 'I'm only her mother when all is said and done. And you can't tell me,' she went on, hardly pausing for breath, 'that this bother hasn't something to do with her having that illegitimate baby all those years ago!'

Never in her whole life had Ann wanted to slap anyone's face as much as she did now. 'Mrs Morgan! You have absolutely no ...'

'There! That shocked you didn't it?' the woman said with satisfaction. 'Told you I could tell you a thing or two.'

'If you set out to shock me, Mrs Morgan, I'm afraid you've not succeeded.' Ann spoke the words between clenched teeth. 'I know about your daughter's illegitimate baby.'

As soon as the words were out, she realized her folly. But turning on her heel, she stormed through the gate, leaving a speechless Mrs Morgan gaping after her.

Ann was quick enough to realize that there was nothing to be gained by lingering here. She needed to get away from this frightful woman who Kathleen Sykes was unfortunate enough to have as a mother.

SEVEN

There was a baby clinic in progress when Ann arrived at the surgery and the noise of crying infants did little to calm her frayed nerves.

'Something wrong, Doctor Davis?' asked one of the two receptionists, looking up from her desk work.

'No. Just a few records I want to look up.'

'Can I help?'

'It's all right, Edith.' Ann willed her not to press further and mercifully the phone rang, demanding all of Edith's attention.

Ann had already had Kathleen Sykes's folder out the previous day to record her admission to hospital, but with both receptionists hovering, she'd not trusted herself to read further back.

Now, so much depended on information which may or may not be here, that her hands shook uncontrollably. If her own birth was not recorded here, then how could she explain to the malevolent Mrs Morgan, if challenged, how she knew of her daughter's illegitimate child?

There were several buff-coloured cards and on the one immediately beneath the current top one, the surname Topham had been scored out and replaced by Sykes. The date, Jan '76 was recorded alongside.

So she'd been Mrs Topham before her marriage to Henry Sykes. If these records were accurate and she'd no reason to believe otherwise, the letter D had been circled in the Marital Status box, indicating she'd been divorced.

The outside edges of the jigsaw were gradually taking shape, but it wasn't this which Ann was searching for just now. In the few entries on the old cards, it seemed that without exception, when

Kathleen had needed a doctor, she'd seen old Doctor Clarke. Struggling to read his spidery scrawl, she worked methodically backwards and came upon brief recordings of the births of her two sons during 1969 and 1970.

'Find what you wanted?' Edith called over.

'Just about.'

'You sure there's nothing I can help with?'

'Not really, Edith. Thanks all the same.' In that instant she realized the records ended. There was nothing before 1968 when, as Kathleen Topham RMN, she'd been treated by Doctor Clarke for 'Bruising to face'.

So her Aunt Brenda had been right. Her mother was a nurse—a registered mental nurse. But Ann's hopes that her own birth would be recorded here, quickly faded.

Carefully she re-read each entry, searching for some clue, some hint that Kathleen Morgan had given birth to a live female in

1955 as she knew to be true from the birth certificate she held. There was nothing. Yet if she'd been listed with another doctor, then such information would have been forwarded when she signed on with Doctor Clarke.

Could the old doctor have withdrawn such information to shield her? Ann knew that hospital staff were often protected in this way for reasons of confidentiality, but was not aware of the procedure in general practice.

What did come to light and trouble her was the nature of her mother's visits to the doctor between '68 and '72. Apart from the antenatal and post-natal visits, there were several which were suggestive of a pattern of events. The 'Bruising to face' entry occurred twice at six-monthly intervals, there was a 'Laceration to eyelid' and 'Sustained blow to right temple', all recorded in Doctor Clarke's spidery scrawl.

Ann didn't at all like the implications of these incidents and was moved to compassion for her mother, at the adversities she seemed to have been subjected to during her life.

'It's for you, Doctor Davis,' Edith's voice broke into her thoughts. 'Mr Kirk on the line.'

'Oh! I'll take it through in my consulting-room.'

'Hi!' came Iain's familiar greeting. 'How's things?'

'Oh fine,' she lied.

'Doing anything special this evening?'

'N ... No.'

'I've two tickets for a barbecue. Care to come?'

'I'd love to.'

'Right. Collect you at eight-thirty. Okay?'

'Yes, yes of course.'

Then he was gone and she was left holding the receiver, bubbles of excitement erupting within her.

The rest of the day flew past and though thoughts of her mother and what she had disclosed to her 'grandmother', rose constantly to trouble her, she pushed them to the back of her mind, just for now.

She'd not looked forward to anything so much for a very long time and found she was laughing to herself with nervous anticipation, as she blow-dried her short hair in front of the mirror.

The door bell rang just as a distant church clock struck the half-hour. Try as she might she couldn't still the churnings of her stomach as she went to open it, nor did they abate at sight of him.

Ann had only ever seen Iain Kirk in formal working suits. Now he wore dark brown cords with a cream, short-sleeved, open-neck shirt which only served to further enhance his dark good looks.

'Hi! Ready?' Before she could answer. 'Mmm,' he nodded his head appraisingly, 'no wonder you're the busiest G.P. in town.'

'Course I'm not.' She laughed, enjoying his flattery.

'How's Mrs Sykes today?' she asked, as

soon as they were in the car.

'Now let's get one thing straight,' Iain replied rather sharply. 'I am off duty and so are you. We make a pact *now*—not to mix business with pleasure.' He took one of her hands and shook it in mock seriousness. 'This evening is for pleasure. Right?'

'Right.' She was stirred by the meaningful look in his eyes. 'Now where is this barbecue?'

'Out in the country near to where I grew up,' he told her, then went on to say how his father had once farmed.

'And what news of your parents in Kenya?' he asked after a while.

She told him as much as she knew from her mother's letters.

'Have you no brothers or sisters?' Iain wanted to know.

'I have one sister, married and living in Bermuda.'

'Is sun-seeking a family trait?'

She laughed. 'We all enjoy the sun, yes,

but in neither case was it solely responsible for the move to foreign parts.'

'So what's your sister doing in Bermuda?'

'Living with her husband as far as I know and working as a receptionist in a hotel.'

'You don't sound terribly sure.' He stole a sidelong glance at her. 'Don't you keep in touch?'

'Only at Christmas and birthdays.'

He laughed softly. 'Sounds a bit like the way I am with my brother.'

'Don't you get on with each other either?'

'Oh we used to! Then ... well ... I suppose you could say something came between us.' He fell silent before adding. 'I've not seen him now for over two years.'

'Is he abroad too then?'

'No. Gavin's an ornithologist working up in Northumberland on the Farne Islands.'

They rounded a bend just then and came upon a cluster of buildings illumined against the darkness of the night. 'This is it,' he told her, slowing down and turning through an open farm gate.

The sound of music reached them as Iain manoeuvred his car into a field to join the lines of parked vehicles. He opened his door and sniffed. 'Smells good anyway. Hungry?'

'Rather!' Ann too had caught the aroma of smoke and singeing meat, overriding the usual farm smells.

Picking up an Aran sweater from behind his seat, he got out, slammed his door and came round to her side.

'I'd better warn you,' he said, a hint of amusement in his voice, 'this crowd've known me for rather a long time, so take anything they tell you with a pinch of salt.'

'Oh?' Ann warmed to his touch as he took her hand and led her towards a large outbuilding.

'I hope you've nothing on that'll spoil,' Iain said, looking her over. 'They're rather a rough crowd, bales of straw for seats and ...'

'Sounds lovely,' she enthused, fascinated now by the scene before her. After climbing some steps, they were on a kind of raised platform running down the centre of the enormous barn, to one side of which were long trestle tables thronged with young folk engrossed in noisy chatter, plates of food and glasses of wine or beer before them. To the other side, the floor had been cleared for dancing and half a dozen couples swayed in unison to a dreamy number.

The whole place was bedecked with brightly coloured bunting and enormous hand-painted posters. There was nothing to indicate that the building had ever been used for the purpose of a barn.

They had joined the end of a small queue for supper. The food was being cooked on large oil drums, cut longitudinally and topped with grids.

'Evening, Iain!' called one of the red-faced cooks. 'Rare, medium or well done?'

'Hi, Ted!' he called back, before turning to Ann.

'Medium,' she mouthed in reply and before long, they were each handed plates with enormous pieces of steak.

'If it's as good as it looks,' Iain shouted above the noise, making his way towards a table of mixed salads, 'it'll be all right.'

Several folk greeted him and more than once Ann was conscious of people looking after him and remarks passed behind raised hands.

There was no room at any of the tables and they were just about to settle for a bale of straw alongside one wall, when someone called his name.

Together they looked in the direction from where the voice had come. A young woman in a red dress, with a sleek bobbed hairstyle, was standing up at one of the tables, poised dramatically with arms outstretched.

Several heads turned in her direction and Ann distinctly heard Iain gasp beside her.

A man sitting beside the girl in red, a dark, bearded, unkempt looking guy, was now on his feet and forcibly compelling his companion to sit down. Ann watched, aware of Iain's taut body beside her as the unkempt man came towards them, seemingly unaware that the girl had risen and was following.

She looked at Iain, expecting some kind of explanation. His face had drained of colour and the muscles in his jaw twitched.

'Iain!' The bearded man had reached them now. 'This is an unexpected pleasure.'

Before Iain had time to reply, the girl in red sidled in between the two men. 'Darling Iain!' she murmured, standing on tiptoe to kiss his cheek.

'Hello, Helga,' he greeted her coolly, before turning to Ann. 'My brother, Gavin.' Here he paused briefly as if searching for the right words before adding somewhat awkwardly. 'And Helga.' Then putting an arm round Ann's shoulder and to the other two, he said, 'Ann Davis—a close colleague of mine.'

Gavin was quick to extend both his

hands to take Ann's. Helga stood her ground and if she made any gesture in reply to Ann's smile of welcome, Ann didn't see it.

'I never thought ...' both brothers began at once, then each laughed, gesturing for the other to go on.

'I was going to say,' Iain began finally, 'that I never expected to see *you* here tonight.'

'The same goes for me.' Gavin laughed. 'Helga's been pestering to come back for ages, but it wasn't until two days since that I knew I could get away.'

'All the time he works,' Helga said petulantly, sidling up to Iain again. 'With you it was different.'

Ann, embarrassed now, watched Iain's lips as he drew them into a firm line. 'Look,' he indicated their plates of food, 'our steaks are getting cold. If you two've eaten, why don't you sample the dance floor while we eat, then we'll get together later.'

Gavin readily agreed, leading Helga away rather roughly, Ann thought.

The steak was succulent and tender but the edge had been taken off Ann's hunger and she ate slowly, acutely aware of Iain's strained mood.

'Your brother's not a bit like you,' she said at last, breaking the silence between them.

'He's not so very different beneath all that hair. Finished?' He put a hand out for her plate.

'Yes thanks. It was delicious ...' her voice faded away as he got up and walked to a table with their plates.

She lost sight of him then for a few moments and when he returned he was carrying two glasses of red wine.

'Helga was once a patient of mine,' he told her unexpectedly, sitting down beside her on the bale of straw.

She looked at him. 'I see.'

'Not half you don't,' he said, with a touch of irony. 'We were engaged. Which is what comes of mixing business with pleasure.'

There was a quiet anger in his voice and Ann didn't know how to interpret it. 'And now?' she prompted carefully, fearful of saying the wrong thing.

'She *types* for my brother. Has done for two years.' He downed his glass of wine and grabbed her hand. 'Come on, let's dance.'

The music playing then was fast, but by the time they'd fought their way to the dance floor, the tempo had changed to a slow beat. She half expected him to wait for another fast piece, instead, he guided her onto the floor then pulled her gently into his arms.

His nearness awakened sensations Ann had never experienced before as together, they moved slowly round the floor. She had often danced with James, but here was something different. She didn't ever want this to end.

When the music stopped, with his arms

still round her waist, he leant back and gazed down at her. 'Had enough?'

'No,' she replied, with no thought of shame.

'Next,' it was Helga's voice right beside her, 'I make request for an "excuse me".'

Ann was startled, but didn't turn and waited for Iain's reply which was slow in coming. 'Unless you stressed "*ladies* excuse me", it will be to no avail.' Then as the music struck up again, he backed away, taking Ann with him.

She smiled to herself, secretly rejoicing in his snub of Helga.

'Excuse me.' This time it was Gavin's voice and his hand was on hers.

She looked up swiftly at Iain. He shrugged resignedly before releasing her to his brother and turning to Helga.

'You might show just a little enthusiasm,' Gavin goaded.

'I'm sorry. I was far away.'

'That's hardly a compliment ...'

'Oh I didn't mean ...' she struggled to

justify her remark, while trying to watch Iain and Helga out of the corner of her eye.

'... at the hospital with my brother?' Ann caught only the end of Gavin's question.

'No. I'm in general practice.' She caught a glimpse of Helga's face upturned towards Iain's, her arms wrapped round his neck.

'You don't need to worry,' Gavin pointed out. 'Iain's pride is too hurt to have her back.'

His perception embarrassed her. Did he mean that Helga was free to return to Iain? That she was nothing to him? Dare she pursue it? Then the moment was lost as someone on the side of the dance floor hailed Gavin and he led her off to meet a group of his old friends.

After what seemed an eternity, they were eventually joined by Iain and Helga, she hanging onto Iain's arm even after they left the floor. Then Iain moved away from her and came to stand beside Ann, slipping an arm loosely round her shoulders.

'You all right?' he whispered close to her ear.

For answer, she merely nodded, just happy to have him by her side again.

'You coming into Hargate to see mother?' Iain asked his brother.

'Oh! Must we?' groaned Helga, before being silenced by a stony look from Gavin.

'I will be,' he replied. 'I gather she's not been too well lately.'

'She's not had a good year,' and Iain went on to detail his mother's health. He had told Ann how, after their father's death, she'd sold up her house and moved into town with him.

'I cannot stay in your house with your mother there,' Helga pouted at Iain, then turned to Ann. 'Can I stay with you in Hargate?'

Before Ann had time to reply, Gavin's eyes blazed angrily. 'You can stay on here at The Dragon. Ann's working full-time, how can ...'

'Oh, it's all right,' Ann offered, feeling

somehow obliged. 'I've plenty of room.'

'Thank you.' Helga flashed her a forced, satisfied smile before turning to Gavin. 'I *must* go to Hargate to see my specialist,' she looked at Iain, 'professionally!'

Two pairs of eyes looked towards Iain questioningly. 'She tells me,' he began rather awkwardly, 'that she's developed a thick band of scar tissue ...'

'Which peeps over her bikini and jeopardizes her chances of returning to modelling. Oh,' groaned Gavin. 'The vanity of women!'

A lovely dreamy number was being played and Ann longed to dance and get away from this uneasy atmosphere, but Iain had different ideas.

'I think we'll get along home,' he said, taking his leave of Gavin and Helga.

'I'll look forward to seeing you in Hargate,' Gavin told Ann, taking one hand in both of his.

'Bye for now, darling Iain,' Helga whispered sensuously, standing on tiptoe and kissing his cheek.

That Iain was disturbed by the meeting with his ex-fiancée was obvious to Ann from his silence on the return journey.

She wanted to draw his attention to the full moon suspended in the night sky like some great luminous ball, but her happiness in his presence had been replaced by an unsettling apprehension, such as one feels on the eve of exams.

As they got nearer to Hargate, thoughts of the practice and its problems, and her sick mother, returned to trouble her. She'd left them all behind for a few brief hours and knew that such switching off, even though spoilt for her tonight, was essential for her survival.

After a long steady climb, they reached the top of a hill where stretched out below them, was the sleeping town of Hargate. Iain braked, bringing the car to a standstill just off the road.

'I feel I owe you an apology.'

'An apology?'

'Well. I've rather landed you in it haven't I? Helga inviting herself to stay with you like that.'

'Oh it's no trouble. There *are* two bedrooms in the flat.'

'Nevertheless, I ...'

'Besides, your brother said he only had four days leave, so it won't be for more than a couple of nights.'

'But didn't he tell you? She's not going back with him.'

'Oh! No. No ... he didn't say.'

'I thought when she said about seeing her specialist, that you would realize. Damn!' He banged one clenched fist into his other open palm. 'I am sorry, Ann.' He turned to face her. 'I wouldn't have had this happen for ...'

'How long ... how long do you think ...?'

'She'll stay in Hargate,' Iain finished for her. 'Heaven knows! She's talking about trying to find modelling work again.'

'I see.' Ann felt trapped, her new-found

happiness crumbling about her. *Was* Iain sorry as he would have her believe, or had he and Helga engineered this arrangement while out there together on the dance floor? Surely not and yet ...'

'Could you drive me home now please? I'm suddenly terribly tired.'

Without replying, Iain started the car and drove off at a great speed towards the lighted town below.

Late though she'd known their return would be, she had planned to ask him in for coffee and had even left the percolator ready just for switching on. Now she couldn't do that. Now things were different.

As soon as he pulled up outside her flat, she reached for the door handle. 'Thanks for a lovely evening.'

'Ann please!' His hand fell on her arm.

'I've a very early start tomorrow ...'

'Look!' He turned her to face him. 'Would you like me to tell Helga it just won't work? Her staying with you I mean?'

'You can't do that. Not now.'

'I could,' he said without conviction. 'It's just ...'

'Leave it for now. If it doesn't work out then she'll not want to stay.'

'I hope you're right,' he said, then cupping her chin in one hand, he brought his lips to rest lightly on hers.

Hungry to feel those lips crushed against hers, she wanted to kiss him back, but her tangled emotions fought off the desire and moving away, she opened the car door and slid from her seat.

'I'll be in touch,' he called after her through the open window.

She didn't trust herself to turn until she'd slipped the key in the heavy front door. He still sat there watching her and she longed, even then, to beckon him in but resolutely moved inside, closing the door behind her.

EIGHT

The day following the barbecue was a very full one for Ann and it was during evening surgery that the phone on her desk rang.

'Doctor Davis. I've Mr Kirk on the line. I'm putting him through.'

'Ann? Iain here.'

'I'm in the middle of surgery. Can you ring me at home?'

'This is strictly business.' There was concern in his voice. 'It's your patient, Mrs Sykes.'

Ann's stomach lurched sickeningly. 'What's wrong?'

'She's refusing to sign her consent form for further surgery and is talking about taking her own discharge.'

'But she can't do that! You can't allow it.'

'There's not a lot I can do about it.'

'But have you told her—she'll die without further surgery?'

'I have and she says unless I can guarantee a cure after this second operation, she wants to spend whatever time is left, at home.'

'But that way, she's throwing whatever chance she has, away.'

'Don't you think I've told her that?' Iain said patiently.

'Of course, I'm sorry. What else can we do?' Ann wanted to tell him 'She's my mother. You can't let her die.'

'We could put her husband in the picture ...'

'But you promised ...'

'Or *you* could try talking to her.'

Ann gripped the receiver. He didn't know what he was saying. 'Is there no-one else?'

'No. And she's scheduled for tomorrow's list.'

So there was nothing else for it. She had

to try. 'I'll come along after surgery,' she told him in a quiet voice.

'That's my girl. By the way, Gavin phoned this afternoon and wants me to find bed and breakfast for Helga. He's bringing her to town tomorrow.'

'Oh, Iain, you can't do that now when I ...'

'We'll talk about it later,' he said firmly. 'Ask Sister to call me when you arrive on the ward.'

Suddenly, the prospect of having Helga to stay was completely overshadowed by the news that her mother, Kathleen Sykes, was risking what chance she had, by refusing this second, vital operation.

Before ringing for her next patient, Ann buried her face in her hands and thought how uncomplicated her life had been before coming to Hargate to search for her natural mother.

Evening visiting was over by the time she arrived at Hargate General Hospital and the car park was nearly empty.

She spotted Iain's blue TR7 parked by the front entrance reserved for senior staff and wished fleetingly that she'd known him longer. Long enough perhaps to have confided in him about Kathleen Sykes. Then he would have understood her predicament and never asked her to assist this way.

Since his phone call, she'd gone over and over what she could say to her mother to convince her that she must consent to this second operation. Now she was here and she still had no idea how she would begin.

The ward was quiet as she entered through the double swing doors and she made for Sister's office where she found her busy at her desk.

'Doctor Davis.' A smile crossed the weary face. 'Mr Kirk said you'd be coming.' She glanced through her observation window and shook her head. 'I don't hold out much hope of you succeeding.'

Ann followed the direction of her gaze

and her eyes fell upon the patient in the second bed on the left. Her face was turned away but she recognized the softly curling, greying hair. 'What is she afraid of?'

'Oh, I don't think fear enters into it—not for herself anyway.' Sister looked up at Ann. 'She's one of the bravest women I've ever nursed.'

Ann swallowed and averted her eyes. Sister was no mean age and must have nursed a fair number of women in her time.

'You said on the phone the other day, that she was fretting ...'

'She still is,' Sister told her. 'Can't bear to be parted from her boys. Oh dear,' she reached for the phone, 'Mr Kirk asked me to call him as soon as you ...'

'Not just yet,' Ann intervened. 'I'd like to try on my own first.'

'All right.' She picked up a folder from her desk. 'They're her case notes.'

While Sister bent again to her work, Ann, her insides churning, carefully turned the pages hoping that she might find here what she had failed to find in the surgery.

Sure enough, the medical facts of her own birth were recorded along with every other ailment or medical condition during her mother's life-time. At least now, if challenged on her knowledge of the matter, she no longer had any fear.

She placed the folder on the desk and slipped quietly out of the office.

Ann had been struck by her mother's spare frame the very first time she'd seen her, but now, the bare jaundiced arms against the stark white of the hospital sheet, appeared thinner than ever. She let her eyes travel upwards, over the pretty cotton nightdress covering the bony shoulders to the scrawny, hollow neck and the pinched face with its sunken, closed eyes.

Her heart twisted painfully. 'Mrs Sykes!' She kept her voice low as she stood by the foot of the bed.

The eyes opened immediately and Ann

saw the startled, haunted look before the light of recognition. 'Doctor Davis,' came the weak voice and she raised a hand in welcome.

Ann had difficulty suppressing the urge to go to her mother and hug her in the way a daughter would. Instead, she took the thin hand and holding on to it, sat in the chair alongside the bed.

'It's nice of you to look in, Doctor.' Mrs Sykes smiled.

'I wanted to see how you were.'

'Sure I'm fine, thank you.' She paused and her eyes misted. ' 'Cept for my boys. I do miss them.'

'They've not been in to see you?'

'Only Sundays they're allowed.' There was a catch in the gentle voice and she brushed a hand across her cheek.

'And how's your husband coping?'

'Henry's marvellous,' she said slowly with surprise. 'Twice today he came in to see me.'

'And your mother?'

Mrs Sykes dropped her eyes and the furrows in her brow deepened. 'She doesn't like hospitals, Doctor. Though she did come that first day,' she added hastily.

'I suppose she's kept busy looking after the boys,' Ann suggested with a benevolence she didn't feel.

'Only another day or two, then she can go back home,' Kathleen Sykes whispered more to herself than to her visitor.

'Who's going to look after them then?' Ann asked, feeling her heart thudding.

'I am, Doctor.'

'But what about your operation?'

'I can't go through with that,' she said, as if she'd been asked to scale the Himalayas.

'But you *must.*' Ann leaned forward and pressed the thin hand.

A brief smile flittered across the patient's face. 'None of you doctors seem to understand,' she said enduringly. 'It's not that I don't appreciate what you're trying to do.' She moved her hand from beneath Ann's and began plucking at the sheets. 'It's just that I want to be home with my boys.'

'But you will be,' Ann told her passionately.

'That's what Mr Kirk says. No, Doctor.' She looked over Ann's head. 'I'm not due another chance.' She smoothed the top sheet now with exaggerated movements. 'There are those who would say I'm only getting my just rewards.'

'How can you talk like that?'

'Oh, my mother's one of them,' she cast her eyes down and her soft voice was barely audible, 'who'd say I was only paying for past sins.'

'No!' Ann was adamant now. 'Life's not like that.'

'Maybe not.' She sank back into the pillows and closed her eyes. 'But there've been events in my life of which I'm not very proud.'

Ann couldn't reply for the lump in her throat was threatening to choke her. She wanted so much to tell this brave woman that that wasn't so—that the baby she'd unselfishly given up all those years ago was now a qualified doctor. An achievement any mother should be proud of.

But would it be right to tell her? What effect would such news have on this woman whose life lay precariously in the balance? Did she want to reveal her identity to benefit her sick mother or herself? She didn't know. But she did know why she was here and she saw with sudden clarity that she mustn't exploit that privilege for her own end.

'Mrs Sykes,' she said, gently but firmly. 'What will happen to your boys when you are no longer here?'

Dark eyes sought hers and for the first time Ann was struck by the likeness to her own. 'When I am ... no longer here?' Each word was spoken slowly as if the full impact of their meaning was just registering.

'Mr Kirk *has* explained,' Ann paused,

reluctant to have to spell it out this way, 'that without this operation, any time you have at home will be a bonus?'

She watched as the dark eyes became liquid before closing, and then flinched as tears coursed down the once plump cheeks. She wished herself dead in that moment, but knew she must go on. 'Your lads, Paul and Ben, you can't walk out on them like that.'

A terrible sob racked the frail body and Ann feared that she had said too much. The small hands on the bed-covers clenched into fists.

'Don't say that, Doctor,' came the distressed request. 'Supposing I agree to this operation and supposing I die having it ... before I get home to my boys?'

'You won't!' Ann covered one of the clenched fists with her hand. 'But all right, to answer your question—supposing you did die—then at least you died putting up a fight. Not this other way—this self-destructive way.'

A clatter of crockery from the ward kitchen was the only sound as Ann, drained now, waited for some response. At first she thought she was imagining it, then very gradually, the fist beneath her hand slowly slackened until finally the fingers opened and clasped hers.

It was a moment she would treasure for as long as she lived. Her mother's ravaged face slackened of tension and the lips moved. Ann leaned closer in order to catch the whispered words.

'Perhaps you're right, Doctor.' Then after a long pause, she opened her eyes and sought Ann's. 'Tell me, why do you care so much?'

'Because you're my mother,' Ann wanted to say as she struggled with a surge of emotion. Instead, she replied, 'Because doctors are trained to save lives.'

'And you think ... this operation to-morrow will save mine?'

'I ...'

'If it's anything to do with me it will,'

came a familiar voice from behind, startling both women.

'Mr Kirk!' Kathleen Sykes said sheepishly.

'Doctor Davis.' He nodded towards Ann before perching himself on the edge of the bed and addressing his patient. 'I've just come from seeing the chief nursing officer about you.'

'About me?' His patient's eyes widened.

'About your sons, to be more precise. She's agreed to bend the rules on visiting.'

'Really? You mean ...?'

'They can come in each day.' He looked from Mrs Sykes to Ann and back again. 'Providing,' here he shook his finger at her, 'that you follow doctor's orders.'

'Oh ...' Her eyes had filled up again and she turned her head away. 'It's ever so good of you ...' Her voice faded away before coming back, a little stronger to say. 'I'd decided to have that operation tomorrow.'

'That's settled then. Come on, Doctor

Davis. Better let our patient get some rest before her big day.'

Ann and Iain made their way back to Sister's office. 'Best get to her with that consent form,' Iain told Sister, 'before she has second thoughts.'

'You mean you've persuaded her?' There was relief in her weary face.

'She persuaded herself in the end,' Ann replied modestly.

After a few exchanges with Sister, Iain took his leave and led Ann off the ward.

'There's some kind of regional administrator's meeting in the Board Room,' he told Ann. 'There's coffee outside, so we'll help ourselves and go on to my office for a chat.'

She put up no opposition. She felt shattered after the ordeal with her mother and could imagine nothing more welcome than a cup of coffee.

The Board Room door was closed but outside was a table upon which stood a large, stainless-steel coffee urn, cups and saucers and two plates of biscuits.

'You sure no one'll object to us taking their coffee?' Ann asked as she watched Iain pour the dark steaming liquid into two cups.

'They're only admin staff,' he whispered. 'Besides, there's enough coffee here for a whole army.'

Even while he was speaking, the Board Room door opened and several men came out. Ann, feeling slightly diffident, stood to one side while one of the men, obviously known to Iain, began chatting to him.

It was just in that moment she caught sight of James and experienced a wave of guilt as he looked her way.

'Ann!' He came straight towards her. 'I'm on my way to see you.'

Immediately, his presumption irritated her. 'How did you know I'd be in?'

'There isn't a G.P. who's on duty *every* evening,' he chided. 'What are you doing here anyway?'

'About to take coffee with me actually,'

Iain told him, stepping up alongside.

James's face clouded and Ann thought for one horrible moment he was going to hit out at Iain. She cleared her already clear throat. 'James,' she began, feeling slightly awkward, 'this is Iain Kirk, one of our consultants. Iain, this is James Divine, Hospital Secretary from St Mark's, where I used to work.'

She watched with baited breath while each looked the other over.

'Pleased to meet you,' Iain said casually, extending a hand in welcome.

James took it. 'Good evening,' he replied icily.

'Now if you'll excuse us,' Iain made as if to go, 'Doctor Davis and I have some business to discuss.'

'Goodbye, James.' Ann smiled kindly at him, as grudgingly, he stepped back allowing her to pass.

'Your male secretary?' Iain quipped, as soon as they were out of earshot.

Partly because of the success with her

mother and partly because of Iain's handling of the meeting with James, Ann felt a little fountain of laughter, but with carefully measured calmness, replied, 'He did take your call to my flat one evening.'

They had reached the deserted Out Patients Department and he pushed open a door for her to enter. 'All hospital secretaries are officious.'

'You can't possibly make such a sweeping statement,' she protested. 'I used to think all surgeons were inhuman!'

'And what do you think now?' He raised his eyebrows at her then firmly shut the office door.

'Now ...' She racked her brains desperately, realizing the trap she'd walked into. 'I don't only think it. I know it!'

Without warning, in one move he put down his coffee cup, reached out an arm and pulled her to him. 'You cheeky young whipper-snapper!' He took her face between his hands. 'I'll teach you.' Then his mouth was upon hers, crushing her to him as she'd longed him to do only the previous evening. Fleetingly, she responded before sanity dawned and she tore herself away.

'How dare you?' Her voice was low and dangerously calm. 'James may be officious as you suggest, but he'd never do a thing like that.'

'I don't suppose he would.' Iain chuckled.

Ignoring his provocation, her emotions now playing havoc with her, Ann moved purposefully to the other side of the desk. 'I thought it was your motto never to mix business with pleasure,' she accused.

'Who said anything about pleasure?'

'Oh!' She stamped one foot in exasperation. 'Then why have you brought me here?'

'To discuss the *business* of Helga.'

'What is there to discuss?'

He walked to the window and stood with his back to her looking out. 'I think it's better if she doesn't come to you.'

'But I've already made up her bed,' Ann lied. 'Besides, if she can't go to your home what *do* you intend doing with her?'

'Find her lodgings somewhere in town.'

'You can't do that. She's your ex-fiancée ... and ... and your brother's secretary.'

He spun round to face her. 'My brother's what did you say? Forget it, you dear little innocent. Right now, she's my brother's nothing.'

Ann knew he was laughing at her expense and resented his manner. Of course she wasn't blind to the way things were, but neither was she insensitive enough to have referred to Helga in any other form.

'Look Iain. I agreed to have her to stay and I'll stand by that.'

'All right.' He put up a hand. 'But don't imagine for one moment that it will be easy.'

She wanted to say, 'You sound as if you should know,' but thought better of it. She looked at her watch. 'Unless there is anything else, I would like to get on home.'

'Of course. You must be tired. If I bring Helga round to your place early tomorrow evening, will that ...?'

'So long as it's after five. Or I could give you a key?'

'No,' he said rather hurriedly. 'I'm not sure that would look too good.'

Ann smiled to herself. Look too good to who? Helga? What was he trying to say?

They made their way back to the Board Room in silence. There was no-one about and they placed their dirty coffee cups along with the others, before heading for the way out.

'Thanks for coming to my aid with Mrs Sykes,' he said, once outside.

'Oh, it was nothing.' She cast her eyes down and with the toe of one shoe, kicked a tiny pebble ahead of her. 'Do you think you might let me know how she gets on tomorrow?'

'Of course.'

They'd reached Ann's car now and after unlocking the door, she turned to him and found he was watching her, his eyes searching hers, a tiny pucker in his forehead.

If only she could tell him. Ann's need to confide in someone—to seek advice as to whether or not she should face her mother with the truth, was becoming unbearable.

Then the moment was lost, as Iain, holding the car door open for her, asked again, 'You're quite sure now—about Helga?'

'Yes I'm sure,' she answered irritably, her mind now full of more important matters.

NINE

Next day seemed to drag, with Ann watching time pass and willing Iain to phone through with a report on Kathleen Sykes. When he didn't, first she told herself he was still in the operating theatre, then she began to fear the worst.

With the episode in her office still causing her mixed feelings, she no longer felt confident at the thought of phoning him, so decided she'd just have to be patient until he arrived that evening.

It was just past six when the bell of her flat door rang.

Opening the door to her visitors and seeing Helga almost dwarfed standing beside Iain, she was struck by how doll-like she appeared. The cheeks of her heavily made-up face were chubbier than she remembered and her lacquered hair was shaped to precision. She held an armful of roses.

'Look what darling Iain has brought me.' She smiled widely at Ann.

'As I pointed out,' he reminded her, 'I brought them for the flat, for you *both* to enjoy.'

'They're lovely,' Ann managed.

'Always he used to bring me roses,' Helga went on, entering the flat as if she were on a cat-walk.

'I've a casserole in the oven,' Ann told them. 'Perhaps you'll stay and have dinner with us, Iain?'

'Oh! But I'm not allowed a casserole,' Helga groaned before Iain had chance to reply. 'I've to lose half a stone before my interview in three days time.'

'Well I'm not dieting and I'd love to stay to dinner,' Iain enthused, dumping two seemingly heavy suitcases unceremoniously. 'Though I could be called away for I am first on call.'

'Always you are working,' Helga pouted.

Ann pointed to the phone. 'You'd better let the switchboard know where you are,' she told Iain.

'I already have.'

'Which is my room?' Helga asked haughtily, as if annoyed that attention was diverted from her.

'I'll show you.' Ann led the way. 'But what am I going to give you for dinner?'

'A dry bone,' Iain suggested, bringing up the rear with the suitcases.

'Not always is Iain very funny,' Helga complained.

'You must start as you mean to go on, Ann,' Iain said authoritatively. 'It's not a hotel you're running. Let her get her own meals.'

'That is no trouble,' Helga was quick to retort. 'Most of my life since leaving school I have prepared my own meals.' She turned angrily to Iain. '*And* yours *and* your brother's!'

Ann was acutely embarrassed and sensed

to her surprise, that Helga was close to tears. There was so little she knew about this young woman. Whatever was she letting herself in for?

'I hope you'll be comfortable here,' she told her, opening the door of the spare room. 'The bathroom's just opposite. If you'd like to unpack ...?'

'Thank you.' Helga, still holding the roses, walked slowly towards the window. 'It is very nice.'

Iain, having deposited the suitcases, was gesturing to Ann to follow him from the room.

'Had a good day?' he asked in a lowered voice, once back in the lounge.

'Not especially.' Then because she couldn't bear the suspense any longer. 'How did it go this morning? Mrs Sykes' operation?'

'Oh that!' He sighed and lowered himself into an armchair. 'Not as well as I'd hoped.' His face was serious.

'Did something go wrong?'

'Not exactly.' He ran his fingers through his hair. 'The whole thing just took much longer than I'd anticipated.'

'Do you think she'll be all right?' she pressed.

'It's never that simple, as you well know.'

'But will she get home?'

'She'll get home.' He opened his hands and shrugged his shoulders. 'For how long, I wouldn't like to predict.'

'Will she have chemotherapy?'

'Sure! That's why I wouldn't attempt a prediction. They're having fantastic results with drugs—in some cases. Now!' He banged the flat of his hand on the chair arm. 'Enough's enough. Business over—pleasure begins.'

Ann couldn't help from smiling despite the feeling of helplessness and despondency over her mother's condition. 'Very well.' She got to her feet. 'A drink before dinner?'

'Sounds grand.'

But Iain never got his drink for he was called away just then and Ann was left to spend the first evening with Helga on her own.

Several days later, Ann was alone in her consulting-room after a heavy evening surgery. Since Helga had moved in, some of the pleasure of returning to her flat had been lost and she was browsing over an article in a medical journal, when she heard someone enter the surgery by the side door.

She held her breath, curious as to who could be around at this time, having called goodnight to their cleaner half an hour ago.

'Anyone here?' came a gruff voice, at once familiar to Ann.

'Yes I am. In here.' She smiled with pleasure as the door was pushed open to reveal the kind-faced, elderly doctor.

'Have you no home to go to?' He peered at her over his spectacles.

'I was just on my way.' She closed the

journal and shuffled the patients' cards into an orderly pile. 'When did you get back?'

'Late last night.' He sat down heavily in the chair across the desk from her.

'But I thought you weren't due for ...'

'Been away long enough. Besides, the courses were teeming with golfers younger and better than me.'

She laughed, remembering her father's attitude to the sport. 'You'll soon get your swing back after a few sessions on the practice tee.'

'Huh!' he grunted. 'Seems from what's been happening here, it was time I got back.' He removed his spectacles and after breathing on them, began polishing them with a handkerchief pulled from his trouser pocket.

'Why? What ...?'

'Heard tell about your bother with the Sykes.' He glowered at her beneath his bushy eyebrows before replacing his spectacles.

'They were no bother. Not for me. But

it must've all come as rather a shock ...'
She stopped in her tracks. 'But how do you know ...?'

'I called in here this morning while you were out on visits. John Currie put me in the picture. I tried to reach you on the phone.' He clasped his hands and leant back in his chair. 'Anyway, I've been to see for myself now.'

'How ... how are things?'

'Henry's not looked better for years—claims it's due to a change of doctor,' he grinned fleetingly, 'and nothing to do with the presence of his mother-in-law.'

'And Kathleen? Have you seen her too?'

'Aye. I've seen Katie.' A great sadness filled his voice and he kept his eyes down, filling Ann with great foreboding. She waited for him to go on.

Finally, after what seemed an eternity, he said, 'You must be thinking what a damn fool I've been not to recognize a sick woman when I see one. Nay, not a sick woman—a dying woman.'

Ann was shocked by his words but could say nothing for fear that words would choke her. Then, summoning all her courage, she began.

'Doctor Clarke. It never even crossed my mind that you had failed to see Mrs Sykes was a sick woman.' With the memory of Iain's words to give her confidence, she added, 'And who says she's dying?'

'It's written on the cards ...'

'Not yet it isn't!' She rose to her feet and stood behind her chair. 'Cancer still claims too many victims, Doctor Clarke, but more and more people are *living* with it and that's what *I* choose to believe.'

'Aye,' he said plaintively. 'I used to be filled with that kind of spirit too when I was younger.'

'Well, that's the kind of spirit we need, to give patients like Kathleen Sykes a chance.'

'Seems to me,' he grinned wryly, 'you've already given her that—you and that young fellow, Kirk.'

189

A warmth crept through her body at his words.

'Full of praise for the pair of you, she is.' He wagged a finger at her. 'I thought I warned you, not to let Kirk have all his own way.'

'But I haven't!' Ann's eyes widened.

'Well see that you don't.' He waved an arm. 'Now sit down and tell me what you make of this.'

Ann sat down and waited for him to begin, curious as to what was coming.

'I suppose you'll know now through taking her case history, that Katie Sykes had a baby out of wedlock?'

Ann's heart was racing, her breath coming in short painful gasps. She could only nod.

'Well it was a baby girl and she'd no choice but to have it adopted.'

Ann could hear a rushing in her ears now and thought her head was going to burst. The old doctor's face was swimming before her.

'Now she's got some silly notion of trying to trace this daughter before she dies,' he was saying.

'Really?' She heard her own voice as if from far away.

'Really,' he echoed, strumming his fingers on the desk and mercifully not looking at her. 'Because I attended at the birth, she's asked me to help her find this lost child.'

'And will you?' The voice was hers and yet Ann's thudding heart was so deafening, she was barely aware of having spoken.

'I don't know.' His strumming became more urgent. 'I don't know. I've told her I won't consider it until she's told Henry.'

'He ... doesn't know then?'

'No. Though how that mother of hers has kept her tongue, I'll never understand.'

Ann had to struggle to think clearly. Her mother, caught as she was in the shadow of death, had expressed a desire to trace her long-since relinquished, illegitimate child. Old Doctor Clarke, her confidant, was questioning the wisdom of her notion.

This last fact helped to steady her nerves and gave her courage to ask something which had puzzled her since she'd first seen the blank space on her birth certificate.

'Was the father of the child not free to marry?'

'That's one way of putting it.' Doctor Clarke stopped his strumming and examined his finger-nails. 'They were engaged to be married when it was discovered he had an incurable disease.' He sighed heavily. 'He never did live to see his child.'

Ann's heart was once more moved to compassion for the suffering her mother had known. 'And yet ...' she began.

'I know what you're thinking.' He banged his fist on the table. 'And yet she gave up his baby.'

'It does seem ...'

'Wasn't so easy for single parents in those days. Her mother'd turned her out and her Gran, who'd taken her in, had a stroke just about the time the baby was born.'

Tears pricked Ann's eyes. She could only swallow and shake her head.

'Katie saw it as her duty to look after her Gran,' Doctor Clarke went on. 'Yes, even at the price of giving up her child.'

After some moments silence, Ann plucked up courage and asked. 'How much does she know—about the people who adopted her daughter?'

'Not much. No names of course. A couple from this county with one child of their own—husband's in the textile trade.'

Ann felt a shiver traverse through her whole body, then Arthur was speaking again.

'Not much of a lead that. Could apply to hundreds.'

Just then the phone at Ann's elbow shrilled noisily, startling her so that her hand shook as she lifted the receiver.

'Ann?'

'What is it, Helga?'

'Are you never coming home this evening?'

Ann smiled. She was getting acquainted with the young woman's mood swings, but the solicitude in her voice was something new.

'Is something wrong, Helga?'

'Nothing is wrong. But your aunt has come.'

'Oh! Tell her I'm on my way and perhaps you'd make her a cup of tea?'

'But I am going out. Now.' There was an air of suppressed excitement behind her words.

'Oh very well. Tell ...'

Arthur Clarke had risen to his feet and was now hovering in the doorway. He raised an arm and mouthed. 'I'm off.'

'Just a minute, Helga.' Ann put her hand over the mouth-piece. 'I am sorry ...'

'No, no.' He dismissed her apology. 'I've kept you long enough as it is.' Then the door closed behind him.

'Helga. You still there?'

'Yes. What did you say?'

'Just tell my aunt I'm on my way. Have a good time and you've got a key so you don't need to rush back.'

'Oh I shall not.' She laughed with a return of her self-assurance.

Iain's brother, Gavin, was due to return to Northumberland. Assuming it was him taking Helga out, Ann was pleased that at least on parting, they were to remain friends. The rift in the couple's relationship on top of Helga's failed interview, had resulted in a moroseness in the young woman which had become an increasing concern to Ann.

Overshadowing all this now was Doctor Clarke's return and all it had brought to light. With her aunt waiting to see her, Ann tried to push the matter from her mind and drove home to her flat.

Pulling in behind the grey Volvo, she couldn't help wondering what her aunt was doing in Hargate so late in the day.

She wasn't kept long in suspense.

'This letter was in the lunch-time post.' A blue aerogramme was thrust into Ann's hand before she'd a chance to take her jacket off.

Her eyes skimmed the brief note.

Mummy suggested Harley Street ... The words screamed up at Ann from the page. She darted a glance at her aunt.

'Oh, read it properly instead of jumping to conclusions.'

Ann returned to the letter and her sister's familiar scrawl.

... She insists on being there so we're both flying into London on the 20th and will take it from there ...

The remaining few lines blurred before her eyes. The twentieth! But that was next week. She put out a hand to the chair near her and sank into it.

'Well?' She felt her aunt watching her. 'What do you think to that?'

'I ... I don't know what to say ...'

'Harley Street!' Aunt Brenda got to her

feet. 'Can you just imagine what that'll cost your parents?'

'I can. And the fares on top ... but it's not so much the cost ...'

'Oh I know,' her aunt intervened, reaching out and taking the letter from Ann. 'She *had* to trouble your mother even though I asked her not to.' She held the letter out and adjusted her spectacles. 'Listen to this last bit. *I feel a baby would be the makings of Rick and me. The doctors here tested us both last year and claim there's no reason why I shouldn't conceive.*'

Aunt Brenda banged down the letter on a chair arm. 'Why can't she be patient? And what kind of a relationship is it that it needs a baby to hold it together?'

'Maybe she's right.' Ann shut her eyes and rested her head back. 'Perhaps a baby of her own would he the makings of her.'

'Well I'm not so sure.' Her aunt picked up her bag from the chair. 'I felt you should know and I didn't want to tell you over the phone.'

'It was good of you to come over. But don't rush off. At least stay and have a cup of tea.'

'I wouldn't say no.' She looked at her watch. 'I don't want to be here though when your flat-mate gets back.'

'Oh, she'll not be back for hours. But why? It wouldn't matter if you were here.'

'I didn't take to her,' Aunt Brenda said bluntly, following her niece into the kitchen.

'Oh?' Ann smiled to herself, well acquainted with her aunt's candour. 'Helga's all right really.'

'All right is she? She certainly knew how to seduce the poor fellow who phoned, into taking her out.' She tutted loudly. 'Tears an' all. No shame, creatures like her.'

'Things are different these days,' Ann said fondly.

'Aye and more's the pity. Now, if you give me a key to your parents house, I'll go over there next week, turn the air around and make up a couple of beds.'

'But mother and Jane may not even come up north,' Ann protested.

'Sure to. Your mother'll jump at the chance of seeing your flat.'

'Do you really think so?' Ann felt no joy, only increased anxiety. She would much prefer to get down to London and keep them away from Hargate just now.

'Stands to reason she'll want to come up. Doing all that for Jane. Hasn't she always endeavoured to treat you both alike?'

Her aunt's words kept Ann awake long into that night. Of course it was true that her mother had always displayed fairness to her daughters in every way. She had been a good mother to Ann in every way possible.

Was she then being a traitor in seeking out her natural mother as she had, against the wishes of Iris Davis, the only mother she'd known?

What of the dangers of Iris discovering any of it if she were to come here to the flat, especially now, with Ann's true identity perhaps on the point of being disclosed?

With clenched fists, she beat her pillow and felt tears of frustration fill her eyes. What was she to do? If she'd not been quite so hasty towards James, despite his opposition to her search, he may have been able to advise her now.

It wasn't James Divine though, who filled her mind as she finally fell asleep, but Iain Kirk, and she dreamt of barbecues, soft lights and music.

With the return of Arthur Clarke and his resumption of duties, Ann no longer had an excuse for visiting either Kathleen Sykes in hospital or Henry and the boys at home.

Until events were clarified one way or the other over the wisdom of her revealing her identity, she knew she should stay away from her mother. Yet it might be weeks before Katie summoned up the necessary courage to tell her husband of her illegitimate baby.

Supposing Doctor Clarke's worst fears were realized? Supposing her fate was written on the cards? That could result in Ann never seeing her again. There had to be some way out of such an appalling prospect.

Returning to her flat next evening, a scent of roses filled the air, so that she looked round expectantly.

'Is that you, Ann?' came Helga's voice from the direction of her room.

'Course it's me,' she replied, a trifle impatient after an exhausting and frustrating day. 'Who else would it be?'

'Oh, who can tell?' She appeared just then in her doorway, beautifully poised on high-heeled sandals, a blue silk dress hugging her figure.

Ann glanced down at her practical, tailored skirt and blouse and couldn't help wondering if she'd look as devastating in the blue dress.

'I thought I could smell roses ...?' she looked around.

'They are in here.' Helga indicated her own room. 'You were in bed when I brought them home last night.' She patted her already, perfectly groomed hair. 'Iain insisted that I bring them.'

So she'd seen Iain last evening too, not that that was surprising, for it was Iain's home where Gavin had been staying.

'Did Gavin get away all right today?' Ann asked.

Helga turned heel into her room. 'I'm afraid I overslept,' she called over her shoulder, 'so I cannot really say.'

Ann put down her black bag, kicked off her shoes, picked them up and plodded thoughtfully through to her bedroom where she undressed before going to take a bath.

Soaking in the deep water, eyes closed, she began to relax.

There came a light tapping on the door. 'Are you in there, Ann?'

She groaned silently and imagined this is what it must be like if she was married with children. Couldn't even take a bath in peace. 'Yes,' she called back with a patience she wasn't feeling.

'There is something I must ask. Will you be a long time in there?'

'Ten minutes maybe, but come on in.'

'The steam, it may spoil my hair. I will wait.'

Ann was unable to suppress the ripple of laughter which escaped her lips and she had to put a hand to her mouth.

Then the phone rang and she made out Helga's footsteps going to answer it. Her hopes soared. Perhaps it was Iain. The thought urged her into action and she was drying herself when Helga called genially.

'I cannot wait, Ann. I am going out. I want to ask to stay six more months with you?'

Ann had been stooping to dry her feet. Now she stood upright and clutched the towel to her. Six more months! Her face in the steamy mirror reflected her sinking heart.

'Ann!' There was an urgency in Helga's voice. 'Are you still in there?'

'Yes ... yes I'm still here. Look, let's discuss this tomorrow ... I ...'

'But I must know tonight. I have a job now.'

'Oh that's nice.' Ann tried to sound pleased. 'A modelling job?'

'No. I am going to be private medical secretary. Now please, Ann, give me your answer.'

Despite the warm, steam-filled room, Ann began to shiver. Warning bells were ringing in her head like noisy alarms. Suddenly her fears mounted and her control began to slip.

'I refuse to make decisions in this manner,' she called. 'Besides, I may need your room for my mother and sister ...' her voice faded as the doorbell resounded through the flat.

'Now I must go,' Helga called. 'But as

Iain says, I do not think you will turn me out.'

Ann sank onto the low stool, the large towel now draped round her and buried her face in her hands. What kind of a person was she, she asked herself? She should have been glad for Helga that she had found work. Glad also, that since yesterday the moroseness had lifted—that things were looking up for Helga. Instead, a deep resentment was growing within her, a resentment grounded on suspicions and yes, she had to admit, on jealousy.

As the flat door banged noisily shut, she was tempted to dash to the lounge window where her suspicions could have been allayed or confirmed. Instead, she sat on until she knew that whoever had called for her flatmate would be well away and out of sight.

For the remainder of that evening, when thoughts of Helga and Iain didn't crowd her mind, then thoughts of her mother did. The thin, lined face of Katie Morgan, framed by the softly curling, greying hair seemed to be everywhere she looked. She saw it in the patterned curtains, she saw it in the pages of her medical journal, she saw it in the shadows of her bedroom. Then she saw it in her dreams, when finally she fell into a troubled sleep.

TEN

Helga wasn't up next morning when Ann rose and being in no mood for further harassment, she skipped breakfast and shut the flat door quietly behind her with a sigh of relief.

She met the postman coming up the garden path. 'You must be Doctor Davis.' A cheery smile broke out on his face. 'First time I've clapped eyes on you since you moved in.'

'Good morning. Nice to meet you.'

'There we are.' He passed her two letters, then scrutinized one on top of his pile. 'I've a registered one here for a Miss Helga Holman, same address.'

'That's right. But give her time to answer for I left her still in bed.'

'Right ho,' he replied brightly, walking

away and mounting the steps. 'Good day to you now.'

'And to you,' she said politely, glancing at her letters and going towards her car. One was from James which she slipped into her bag, the other from her parents in Kenya, which she slit open eagerly.

It was in her mother's handwriting and was much as she expected. It told of Jane's failure to conceive and of arrangements for the Harley Street appointment.

Will be up to see you she read *just as soon as any investigations are through* ...

'Here! Doctor Davis!' It was the postman coming towards her, holding out the registered letter. 'Would you sign for this? I can't rouse her for love nor money.'

Ann obliged, then as he walked away, she frowned. Helga wasn't usually difficult to rouse. Recalling the young woman's moroseness earlier in the week, she felt a wave of anxiety.

Cursing at the delay, she got out of her car and dashed back into the house and up the two flights of stairs. 'Helga!' she called out but received no answer. There was no answer to her knocking, so pausing only briefly, she turned the handle on the bedroom door.

Whatever she had imagined, the neat, made-up bed only increased her alarm. She glanced quickly round the room for some clue to Helga's absence. There was nothing.

It was only when she went through to the kitchen that she saw the note sellotaped to the kettle. She crossed to it, her insides churning.

Ann. You were in bed when we looked in. Iain is on call but his mother is unwell. I shall sleep there tonight. Helga.

Angry tears welled up in her eyes. Relief that she'd not done anything foolish as Ann had feared, was swamped by an overwhelming flood of jealousy. Tossing the letter down, she stormed from the flat, banging the door noisily behind her.

Her sanity had been fully restored by

the time she reached the surgery. She told herself that she ought to have known better at her age, than to have fallen under the spell of someone like Iain Kirk.

It was lunch-time before she gave another thought to the letter from James. In the quiet of her consulting-room, still too angry to return to her flat and risk confronting Helga, she opened his letter.

Ann Dear,

I'd like to think that your recent, un-characteristic manner has been due to the unsettling facts surrounding your origins, which prompted your move to Hargate. Perhaps I showed less understanding than I ought. Forgive me please for that.

I have been short-listed for a job in London. Something you know I have long cherished.

If you could see your way to a future with me, I'm sure your partners would release you from what I understand, is not yet a binding contract.

If your reply should be in the affirmative, you would make me a happy man. If in the negative, I feel it better if we do not meet again.

With deep affection, James.

Ann brushed a hand across her cheek and sniffed noisily. Hardly a passionate proposal and the style reminded her of some published letters she'd once read from the last century. Yet the kindness and concern and the prospects of a stable relationship reached out to her now, when she most seemed to need it.

What after all was there to keep her in Hargate? Unless present circumstances altered, she would be denied regarding Katie Sykes as her mother. The situation could become unendurable. Perhaps her future lay in the contents of this letter from James.

Helga was watching television when Ann returned to her flat late in the day. She got to her feet instantly.

'You must have a cup of tea,' she called, heading for the kitchen. 'Afterwards I shall make dinner for us.'

Ann looked after her slightly bewildered. The transformation was a little difficult to swallow.

'I know you are on call,' Helga said, returning with a tea tray, 'so we shall eat at a time convenient to you.'

'Why thank you.' Ann had already decided she would make no reference to the alarm Helga had caused her this morning. Her attitude now however, rather than appeasing her, was having the opposite effect. The young woman was like the two proverbial cats. Not only had she licked the cream, but she'd also caught the mouse. Must she make it so obvious?

'It was not very clever of me,' Helga was saying, 'disturbing your bath last evening.'

Ann had the distinct feeling they were Iain's words. That was just what he would have said if Helga had told him about the incident.

'Can we just leave that for a few days,' she suggested, thankful that the phone should ring just then.

'That you, Ann? Arthur Clarke here.'

'Yes. What can I do for you?'

'A couple of things. I've a letter here which should have come to you. About Mr Wood.'

'Mr ... Wood ...?'

'Old Charlie, from Park Close.'

'Oh yes. The stroke patient.'

'That's him. Due home Friday, so you'll need to put him on your home visits. The other thing,' he paused before going on, 'is about Katie Sykes.'

'Oh yes?' Her heart pounded painfully. 'How is she?'

'Seems to be making some improvement.' There was disbelief in his voice.

'Really?'

'Aye. Anyway, she says how she hopes she's not seen the last of you just because I'm back. Not sure,' he chuntered, 'if she wasn't trying to nudge me out of the business altogether.'

Ann laughed nervously. 'I'm sure she wasn't.'

'She'll not succeed. Anyway, you might look in on her when you've a minute.' Then added as if as an afterthought. 'Purely social of course.'

It was two days later when Ann found herself going through the main swing doors at Hargate General Hospital.

Sister on Female Surgical recognized her immediately. 'Doctor Davis.' She smiled a welcome. 'Mr Kirk and I were only talking about you.'

'Oh?' Ann looked questioningly in the direction of her office.

'He's not around just now ...'

'I hope it was nothing detrimental ...'

'Of course not,' the older woman assured her. 'We were just talking about G.P.s in general and your name came up.'

Of course, Ann thought bitterly, to Iain Kirk she was just another G.P., 'I called in to see Mrs Sykes.' She lowered her voice. 'How is she?'

Sister raised both hands and crossed her

fingers. 'If she continues this way, she could be home in another week. Thanks mainly to you,' she widened her eyes, 'for persuading her to have that second operation.'

'Oh nonsense! All right if I go in?'

'Of course. She'll be pleased to see you.'

Before pushing open the side-room door, Ann peered through the porthole window. Her heart quickened at the sight of Katie Sykes. Both Doctor Clarke and Sister had said there was some improvement, yet to Ann she looked just the same.

She lay quite still against a mound of pillows, eyes closed, head to one side. Ann studied the bare, jaundiced arms, the bony shoulders and scrawny neck, searching for some sign of the improvement.

Then in a moment she saw it. While she watched, her mother's eyes opened, the head lifted from the pillows and it was like a light being switched on. Something enigmatic had entered those features transforming them so that the pinched look was gone, the sunken eyes less apparent.

Ann pushed open the door. 'Hello, Mrs Sykes.'

'Doctor Davis!' She extended both her hands in obvious delight. 'What a lovely surprise.'

Instantly, any awkwardness was gone and it took Ann all her time not to move into the embrace those arms invited. Instead, she clasped both hands in hers.

'You are looking better.'

'And feeling it too,' Katie enthused, then turned towards her laden locker-top. 'It's all these cards and flowers. Can you believe that so many folk should care about me?' A catch had entered her voice and releasing one of her hands, she fumbled beneath her pillow, brought out a tissue and blew her nose.

'Of course I can, Mrs Sykes.'

'Doctor Davis,' she smiled and her eyes were very bright, 'I do wish you would call me Katie. Mrs Sykes sounds so ... so formal.'

'Why yes,' Ann assented willingly. 'I'd love to call you Katie.' She felt strangely flattered at the request and experienced a quiet pride that this woman was her mother.

'Look at this one.' Half laughing, half crying, Katie leaned over and picking up a card, passed it to Ann. 'From the staff at The Haven.'

'That's in York isn't it?'

'That's right. It's the small, private psychiatric hospital where I used to work.'

The card was one of the comic variety and displayed a nurse descending upon a patient with an enormous syringe. Ann grinned. 'Whoever sent you this had a sense of humour. How long since you worked there?'

'Not since I married Henry.' She began to count on her fingers. 'More than six years now.' Then she looked sharply at Ann. 'You know Henry's my second husband—not the father of my boys.'

She said it so naturally that without thinking, Ann found herself asking, 'Do the boys still see their father?'

'Oh no, Doctor!' Katie made no attempt to conceal her dismay.

'I'm sorry. I thought perhaps ...' Ann was sorry now that she'd asked, fearful of what she may have uprooted.

Katie was ringing her hands, her eyes down. 'You see ...' she began, then it was as if she couldn't go on.

Ann hated herself for being the cause of this upset. 'I am sorry.' She put her hand over Katie's. 'I shouldn't have asked.'

'You weren't to know, Doctor.' She passed a hand across her forehead. 'But Rodney's a sick man you see. A very sick man.'

Ann squeezed the hand beneath hers. 'Please don't feel you have to explain, Katie.'

'I'm all right now.' She managed a weak smile. 'I'd like to tell you.'

Ann remained silent. She was recalling the facial injuries in Katie's old notes and half anticipating what was to come.

Raised voices broke out just then outside the door and both women turned their heads expectantly, but no-one entered and the voices faded away until all was again quiet.

'Rodney was one of my patients when I first met him.' Katie plucked at the bedclothes. 'And a violent one at that.' She took a glass of water from her locker-top and raised it to her lips. 'By the time we married, everyone believed him cured.'

Ann said nothing, knowing that Katie would tell her in her own time.

'After the children were born ... well, he began to show the classic symptoms again.' She looked directly at Ann. 'You know about psychiatry, you must understand.'

Ann nodded. 'It must have been very hard for you.'

'It was.' She looked towards the window. 'But so much worse for Rodney. He couldn't help himself.'

Ann cried silently in her heart. 'Oh mother! You poor, brave darling.' 'I'm sorry,' she managed in a soft, strangled voice.

'And now,' Katie went on, examining her fingernails, 'he's in a long-stay hospital and has forgotten there ever was a Kathleen Morgan in his life or even that he was once married, let alone fathered two boys.'

'And the boys? Do they know about their father?'

'As much as they can understand at present.' She ran her fingers through her soft, grey curls. 'Doesn't seem fair on them does it—to lose their dad like that—then this?' She opened her hands and shrugged her shoulders in a sad little gesture.

'But you're improving,' Ann told her. 'Why, Sister's just told me, you could be home in another week.'

'Yes.' Her eyes lit up. 'And that's more than I dared believe a little while ago.'

She sighed deeply. 'Mr Kirk says I shall have to attend Fullbeck from time to time.'

'That's right, but you probably won't need to stay overnight.'

'It's not that.' She frowned. 'It's just that everyone knows it's the cancer hospital. You see ... Henry doesn't know yet ... I ...' her voice faded away.

Ann pondered. 'Don't you think he should know, Katie? That he'd want to share the burden with you?'

'I'd rather he didn't have to.' She spread her thin fingers out and smoothed the sheets. 'You see ... he's put up with so much.' She looked up at Ann. 'Oh I know people think he's a real tyrant, but he's not you know.' Her face softened before resuming a worried expression.

'I still feel you should tell him,' Ann urged gently.

'He has a big enough shock coming to him, Doctor, as it is.'

Ann's mouth went suddenly dry. She

shifted uneasily in her chair. 'How ... how do you mean?'

The door burst open just then and a trolley appeared laden with clean linen followed by a nurse pushing it.

'Wash time, Mrs Sykes. Oh!' The nurse put a hand to her mouth at sight of Ann. 'I'm sorry. I didn't know there was anyone ...'

'It's all right.' Ann rose quickly to her feet. 'I was just going.' She leaned over and touched Katie's cheek with the back of her hand.

'Bye, Doctor.' She smiled wistfully. 'Thanks for listening.'

'I'll try and look in again.' Ann paused by the door, reluctant to leave her mother.

'I'd like that,' Katie whispered in reply.

Ann was making her way out of the hospital and had just passed a lift shaft when she heard her name being called. No sooner had she turned than she wished she hadn't. Iain Kirk had just emerged from the lift. 'Hi. You here to bring me more trouble?' he challenged, his eyes full of laughter.

'More?' she replied defensively. 'I wasn't aware I'd ever brought you *any*.' She struggled to crush the emotions aroused at sight of him.

'What ho?' he chirped, falling in alongside her. 'You're edgy. Is something wrong?'

'Nothing except that I'm running out of time.' She looked pointedly at her wrist watch. 'It's not everyone who can afford a private secretary.' As soon as the words were out, she hated herself for being so churlish.

Iain stopped in his tracks, threw back his head and laughed. 'I do believe you're jealous,' he accused, making no effort to lower his voice so that two nurses approaching grinned at each other.

Ann longed for the ground to open and devour her. Instead, once the nurses were out of earshot, she turned on him. 'If you must make a spectacle of yourself, please leave me out of it.' Then she deliberately quickened her pace so that she left him behind.

Her head was thumping, her insides churning, for despite what she'd said she knew it was her and not him who'd made a spectacle of themselves. 'You fool,' she muttered impatiently with inner fury.

All that week Ann was on tenterhooks, half expecting Arthur Clarke to contact her with news that Henry Sykes had been told about his wife's illegitimate child and that the search was on.

By the morning of the nineteenth she had heard nothing, nor had she returned to visit Katie, and it was this that troubled her most as she drove, in mid-afternoon, to visit Mr Wood at Park Close.

It was partly the pending visit of her adoptive mother which had kept her away from Katie. That, and the fear of becoming too attached.

The fear arose from the fact that she was

still considering James's proposal. If she accepted, it would mean a total severance from Hargate and from Katie.

Pulling up outside Mr Wood's house, she was surprised when two heads peered over the hedge at her.

'Good morning, Doctor Davis,' they chimed in unison.

She pushed the gate open. 'Paul and Ben Sykes! What are you doing over here?'

'Some gardening for old Mr Wood,' the older of the two said, leaning his weight on a garden fork.

'It's me does all the work,' Ben complained, sticking his thumbs inside the waist of his old jeans. 'He,' pointing to Paul, 'bosses me.'

'That's not true,' Paul protested.

'Oh come on,' Ann coaxed. 'You're too big for silly arguments.'

There followed mumbled grunts from both lads then each took a playful swing at the other before returning to their tasks.

Ann was just about to ask how their

mother was when the front door opened and Miss Wood called 'Break time, boys,' then catching sight of Ann 'Doctor Davis. Come along in.'

Ann found Mr Wood sitting in a chair by the window overlooking his garden. He gave her a lop-sided smile as she entered.

'It's lovely to see you back here,' she told him.

'Dad's not talking again yet.' His daughter went to stand beside him and placed a hand on his shoulder. 'He will be though before long.'

'I'm sure he will,' Ann agreed. 'I'll just take a look at you, Mr Wood—check your blood pressure and listen to your chest.'

By the time she took her leave she was satisfied that Miss Wood, with professional help of course, was managing her father superbly.

Katie's two boys had their heads together on the far corner of the lawn as Ann made her way down the garden path.

'Let's tell her,' she heard as she got nearer.

'Everything all right?' she called over

'Yes.' Ben, the younger, eyed her carefully for a moment then demanded urgently. 'Can you keep a secret?'

She smiled. 'I have to keep lots in my job.'

'Cross your heart then and wish to die,' Ben ordered, coming towards her followed closely by Paul.

Fascinated by their game of make-believe, she put down her bag on the path, glanced surreptitiously towards the house and crossed her hands over her chest.

'All right, Paul.' Ben nudged his brother. 'You can tell her now.'

'A long time ago,' Paul began, his eyes feverishly bright, 'our Mum had a baby ...'

'A girl!' Ben interrupted, curling his top lip.

'Our Mum couldn't look after the baby

because her Gran was very ill,' Paul continued with excitement as if his brother hadn't spoken.

But Ann's legs had turned to fluid and she felt sick and faint—terribly faint. She sank to her knees on the lawn and the cold of the grass served to revive her. She forced a smile at the two boys now crouched on the grass beside her.

'How do you know all this?' she asked, her heart pounding until she felt it would burst.

'Dad told us,' Ben confided importantly. 'Last night.'

'And now Mum wants to try and find this lost baby.' Paul's eyes were like stars.

Ann was suddenly overwhelmed by the enormity of the situation. These two boys of course were her half brothers. So Katie had told Henry. She felt strangely exposed for there were no longer any barriers to prevent her revealing her true identity—except Iris Davis, her adoptive mother.

Was Ann able to come to terms with that? Was she ready to accept this family as part of her own? She felt the boys watching her, waiting for her reaction.

'Remember,' Ben threatened, his eyes wide, 'you'll die if you tell.'

'Oh I'll not tell,' she promised, and thought of the mother who'd brought her up arriving in London next day and in Hargate, probably a few days later.

Why, Ann asked herself for the hundredth time, had she been so opposed to any contact between mother and daughter? What possible threat could Katie and her tragic life hold to Iris Davis?

'Isn't it exciting!' Paul brought his face close to hers.

'Oh yes!' she managed.

'It's like a detective story,' he went on.

'Watch out!' Ben pushed at his brother. 'She's coming.'

As all three scrambled to their feet, Miss Wood, carrying a tray, came towards them from the side of the house. 'You still here, Doctor Davis?'

'I'm just on my way.' She smiled at the boys and made for the gate.

'Quite forgot about your refreshments,' she heard Miss Wood say, 'with Doctor arriving like that.'

As Ann approached traffic lights on the way home, she slowed down until amber, then green appeared, changed gear and picked up speed to take her across.

She was still thinking of the meeting with her half brothers when she heard the screech of brakes, the rending of metal—then came the terrible thud and the searing pain before she sank into a deep, bottomless world of darkness.

ELEVEN

The blaring of sirens penetrated Ann's subconscious and through a haze of dark discomfort she became aware of strong arms lifting her.

'Easy Jo,' came a gruff request above the background noise.

She opened her eyes and struggled to get her surroundings into focus. 'What ... what's happened?' she managed. She moved her hands to hold her head and became aware of a sharp pain in her chest.

'Try to keep still,' came the gruff voice and Ann saw now it belonged to one of two, uniformed ambulance men. 'We'll soon have you to hospital.'

'You've had a smash,' came a stranger's voice. 'Some fool who came through the lights at red.'

'Oh!' she groaned, as she was lifted and carried into an ambulance.

'I'll follow in my car,' she heard the stranger say before another wave of darkness overcame her.

Next thing she knew, the doors of the vehicle were thrown open and she was being wheeled from the ambulance through Casualty and into a cubicle, where a doctor and a nurse appeared at her side.

'How much can you remember?' The doctor had his fingers on her pulse as he spoke, while the nurse was putting a cuff on her other arm to take her blood pressure.

'I saw it all,' came a voice from behind the curtain. 'Wasn't this young woman's fault at all.'

Ann succumbed then to a careful and thorough examination, while the unknown witness filled in what details he had of the accident.

'Better have skull and chest X-rays,

Nurse,' the doctor said, then to Ann 'You realize we'll be keeping you in. At least for a few days.'

'Oh but ...' she tried to raise herself to protest, but the pain in her chest was too much and she knew she was too weak to object.

The nurse then wanted all sorts of information—name, age, address and had reached 'next of kin'.

'My parents,' Ann told her, 'though right now, they're in Kenya, at least Dad is, Mum's on her way home.'

'Would you like us to contact them for you?' the doctor offered, as he was about to take his leave.

'No. I'd rather they didn't know.'

'But surely,' the doctor insisted, 'if you say your mother's on the way home, isn't it better if we warn her ...?'

'Oh dear,' she groaned, feeling wretched. 'Can we just leave it for now?' Perhaps tomorrow they would allow her home.

'We do need someone we could contact,'

the nurse insisted, 'just in case ...' her voice faded away.

'I've an aunt and uncle who live near York,' Ann relented, her chest sore just with the effort of talking.

That seemed to satisfy the nurse who didn't pursue her for any more information once she'd got Aunt Brenda's name and phone number.

The trip on the trolley to X-ray did little to improve Ann's discomfort and she was feeling a little sorry for herself when, the X-rays completed, she realized to which ward she was being admitted. Female Surgery—where Katie Sykes was! Only then did the meeting with Paul and Ben come rushing back.

A staff-nurse was beside her now in the corridor of the dimly-lit ward. 'Hello.' She smiled, then turned to the porter. 'In here.' Then led the way to a lighted side-room where she helped lift Ann into the prepared bed.

'The consultant's on his way,' she told

Ann, 'and will prescribe something for those cracked ribs.'

So they were fractured. 'How many?' she asked, sinking back against the mound of prepared pillows.

'Three I'm afraid. X-ray have just phoned through.'

'And my skull?'

'Nothing apparent, but they're sending them up for Mr Kirk to see.'

'Let's have them then.' The command came from the doorway and then he was there in the side-room, his face like his voice, unusually stern.

With a hasty glance at Ann, the staff-nurse scurried out.

'This is your second accident,' Iain said severely, 'in a very short space of time.'

She shut her eyes and bit on her bottom lip. 'It wasn't my fault,' she protested, feeling her eyes filling.

'I never suggested it was.'

She heard the sound of pages turning and assumed he was looking through her notes. His apparent lack of concern was worse than her pain and she couldn't check the tears which flowed uncurbed down her cheeks.

Then she felt his hand on hers. 'I'm sorry! Heaven knows ...'

'The skull X-ray, sir.' It was the staff-nurse's voice.

'I'll see it in the office.' His hand left Ann's and his footsteps receded from the room.

'What's biting him tonight?' Staff-nurse whispered while with expert deftness, she began undressing Ann. 'We must've disturbed his evening.'

Unable to stop her thoughts turning to Helga, Ann felt the nurse probably wasn't too far from the truth.

It was some time before Iain came back by which time, Ann was adorned in a white, hospital gown.

'You're luckier than you can imagine.' He stood at the foot of the bed, his voice still stern. 'The skull X-ray's clear.'

'Thank God!' Without meeting his eyes she said 'I ... I would like to go home tomorrow.'

'No way!' he stated emphatically.

'But ...'

'No buts. You're staying right where you are.'

How could she tell him that she couldn't risk her mother coming here? That she couldn't risk a meeting between Katie Sykes and her adoptive mother?

She risked a glance in his direction to find he was writing on her chart. 'She's to have this injection *now*.' He passed the chart to the nurse. 'I'll wait here while you fetch it.'

'My mother,' Ann began, then paused to gain strength to continue, 'she ... she'll try to phone me at the flat. She arrives in London tomorrow.' She struggled to sit forward. 'I ... I don't want her to know.'

'I can't see why. But okay, you'd like Helga to be briefed. Is that it?'

'Please,' she whispered.

'You're not in when your mother phones. That the sort of thing?'

'Yes but I can't ... I can't put her off after tomorrow. You will let me go home then?'

'I'll allow you home only when I see fit.'

Ann felt too weak still to argue her case further and staff-nurse was back now with her injection. Iain watched in silence while the girl rubbed the skin of her upper arm before plunging the needle home.

It wasn't long before she could breathe without it hurting and as her eyelids became heavy, she could just make out Iain's voice whispering to the nurse.

Several times during the course of that night, she stirred to find someone at her side, checking her blood pressure, shining a torch into her eyes, or pressing sips of water on her.

The first time she roused properly, was to find day Sister standing over her. 'Well, Doctor Davis. You have caused a stir.'

It took Ann several seconds to orientate herself. 'I'm sorry. How ... how do you mean?'

'All your friends phoning in.' Sister plumped up her pillows.

'But how ... how do they know?'

'Local radio. How are you anyway?'

'Better I think.' Ann moved her head to check if the awful ache had gone. 'My ribs are still sore though.'

'I bet they are.' Sister offered her a glass of water. 'I promised all enquirers,' she took a piece of paper from her pocket, 'that I'd tell you who'd called.' She began to read 'Doctor Clarke, Sister June Row, a Miss Wood, Councillor Sykes,' here she raised her eyebrows and grinned, 'James Divine, Doctors Murdie and Currie, and your Aunt Brenda, who is on her way to see you.'

'Aunt Brenda is?' Ann was a little confused by the list of names.

'Yes. I told all the others that there'd be no visiting today.' She then explained to Ann that the physiotherapist would be along to encourage deep breathing and left her with the promise of a cup of tea.

It wasn't long before she put her head round the door again. 'Mrs Sykes has heard you're in here. She's rather upset and wants me specially to tell you she hopes you'll soon be better.'

How like her, Ann thought. 'You've told her I'm all right—that it's nothing serious?'

'I have, but I'm not sure she believes me.'

'How is she? It's several days since ...'

'Mmm, I don't know.' Sister's face took on a puzzled expression. 'Some days she looks great—other days ...' She pursed her lips and shook her head. 'She is up and about a little now.'

Ann hesitated only briefly. 'If she's up and about, perhaps she'd like to come and see for herself that I'm all right.'

'We'll see.' Then she turned at the

sound of voices in the corridor outside. 'Oh! Mrs Davis!'

Ann's heart lurched sickeningly. Her mother was here, but how ...?

'Your first visitor,' Sister announced, holding open the door.

At sight of Aunt Brenda, relief flooded through Ann. She'd quite forgotten that *her* name was Davis too.

'Well!' Her aunt stood there, hands on hips. 'What a time to choose to have your accident.' She came further into the room and peered at Ann. 'At least you're not swathed in bandages from head to foot.'

Ann smiled. 'It's good of you to come, Aunt.'

'Your mother'll have a heart attack when she hears of this.' She lowered herself into the chair by the bed.

'She's not going to hear of it.'

'Oh? And how d'you work that one out?'

'I'll be back at the flat before she comes up north.'

'I thought Sister said you'd cracked your ribs as well as bumping your head.'

'I have.'

'Huh! You doctors! Think you know it all,' she scoffed. 'When my John broke his ribs playing rugby, it was weeks before he was right—weeks I tell you.'

'Yes, well ...'

'*And* they strapped them up in those days,' she added with scorn. 'I believe it's not fashionable now.'

'They realize now that the ribs either side make perfectly good splints.'

'All these new-fangled ideas. Anyway, I'm glad the other driver's admitted all blame.'

'Whoever told you that?'

'The porter who brought me up here. After what happened to your mother, I think another dose of that might have killed her.'

'What did happen to my mother?' Ann asked carefully.

'You don't mean to tell me you don't

know about her accident?'

Ann shook her head and studied her aunt's face.

'Well I'll be ... Have you never wondered why she hates the idea of you driving or why she no longer drives herself?'

'I didn't know she'd ever driven.'

'Oh lor!' Her aunt scratched her head and had that same bewildered expression that Ann remembered from the time she'd let slip the fact that her natural mother had been a nurse.

'Please tell me.'

'I don't know as how I should. Your mother's always been that ashamed.'

'Of what?' Ann urged, determined now to get to the bottom of this.

The door opened just then and Iain Kirk entered followed closely by Sister who turned to Aunt Brenda.

'Mrs Davis, would you mind waiting outside while ...?'

Iain waved a hand. 'No need, no need.' He turned to Ann, his eyes wide with surprise. 'Your mother?'

'My aunt,' she corrected him.

'Mrs Davis.' He stepped forward and took her hand. 'How do you think your niece is then after her escapade?'

Ann watched her aunt succumb to his charm. 'Much better than I expected,' she said, getting to her feet. 'Now you carry on, Doctor, I've got to get back to the farm now anyway.'

'Your husband a farmer, Mrs Davis?' Iain stood a good head and shoulders above her. In thoughtful mood he raised a hand to his mouth. 'Not John Davis ... from somewhere near York?'

'Why yes,' she beamed. 'Do you know him?'

'Not exactly, but I remember my father speaking of him. Didn't he used to take away the annual prize for the best potatoes?'

'He did!' She threw her shoulders back proudly. 'And still does.'

'Pipped my father at the post many a

time I seem to remember.'

'Well I never.' She shook her head in disbelief. 'Wait while I tell my John. Who did you say you were?' She gazed up, eyes shining into Iain's face so that Ann had to put a hand to her mouth to stop from laughing.

'I didn't as a matter of fact,' he teased.

'Mr Kirk,' Sister provided with measured patience.

'Not doctor?' There was disappointment in Aunt Brenda's voice.

'He's a surgeon, Mrs Davis,' Sister explained. 'All surgeons are known as Mister.'

'I see. A surgeon!' Now there was awe in her voice. She went towards the door. 'It's been nice meeting you.' Then as if she'd just remembered her niece. 'Oh Ann! I'll look in again dear. I can see you're in good hands.' With a last admiring glance at Iain, she was gone.

'Small world isn't it.' He took hold of Ann's feet through the bedclothes and with head to one side, looked at her properly for the first time since entering the room. 'You look better. A lot better.'

'Can I ... can I go home then?'

'Indeed you cannot. I might be a campaigner for early discharge but no way are you going home before you're fit.'

'But that could be ages.' She searched his face for understanding.

'Could be.' There was laughter in his eyes. 'We're not in any hurry for this bed are we, Sister?'

'Not at present, sir.' Then she turned in answer to a sharp knock on the door. She opened it and after an exchange of words re-appeared with a large bouquet of flowers. 'Special delivery. Aren't they glorious.' She placed them across Ann's lap.

The few words on the card were brief and as Ann read them she felt Iain watching her. 'These come with my love. Until we meet. James.' She re-read them putting off the moment she'd have to look at Iain.

'We'd better get on, Sister and leave Doctor Davis here with her flowers for therapy.' There was mockery in his voice.

In an effort to hit back, Ann said brightly. 'They're from James Divine, Sister. You'll remember he phoned earlier.'

'Why yes,' Sister recalled. 'The polite young man, insistent I let him visit just as soon as ...'

'Perhaps tomorrow?' Ann suggested.

'I don't see why not.' Sister moved the flowers to straighten the bedclothes.

Iain had opened the door and was tapping one foot impatiently. Ann still didn't trust herself to look at him and as the door closed behind them she sank dejectedly back against the pillows.

She tried to turn onto her side but her chest was too painful. Iain's off-handedness towards her hurt deeply. There'd been a moment last evening when he'd placed his hand over hers, that she'd thought he may feel something for her after all—now she was sure he didn't.

What had her aunt been about to tell her when he'd come into the room? What was this about her mother's accident? Was it in some way tied up with Katie?

Her head was hurting again with trying to work it all out. She closed her eyes. Rain splashed against the window and there was the sound of tyres on a wet surface. Somewhere a phone was ringing. Gradually, these background sounds became fainter until she felt herself drifting off into a deep sleep.

When she awoke it was with a start and she was immediately aware that there was someone in the room with her. She felt the light touch of a hand on her arm. 'It's all right. It's only me.'

'Katie!' Ann tried to raise herself but the pain caused her to fall back against the pillows and she couldn't stop the groan that escaped her lips.

'He should be hung, that driver should, causing you pain like that.'

'Oh it's nothing really,' Ann protested,

ashamed that after all Katie had been through, she herself couldn't hide her discomfort.

A comfortable silence fell between them and it was some time before Katie began. 'I did like you said and told Henry—about having to go to Fullbeck.'

'You did! How did he take it?'

'That well, I think he must've known.'

'Perhaps.' Ann nodded, moved by her mother's calm acceptance.

'It sort of paved the way for what I had to tell him next.'

'And that was?' Ann prompted, for the first time feeling no fear, no apprehension, but the same tiny bubble of excitement that she'd first experienced when she'd begun her quest several months ago.

'That somewhere,' Katie spoke in a hushed voice, 'is a young woman who was once my daughter.' She drew in a long deep breath which escaped as a sigh. 'I had to give her away.' She pulled her flimsy housecoat across her knees. 'But there's never a day of my life that I haven't thought of her.'

Ann's whole body was now so taut, the knuckles of her hands so white, that she had to will herself to relax, to unwind, so that she might be able to say something.

Then Katie was talking again. 'I've told Henry that I want to find that young woman now, before it's too late.'

'Why ... why are you telling me all this?' Ann was wary, for the first time suspicious that Katie might know ... might know who she was.

'Why?' Katie echoed as if surprised. 'Because ... well because you're the kind of person to understand.'

'I'm here, I'm here,' Ann wanted to cry out, 'you've found me', but still filling her mind was the thought of her adoptive mother and her fears and opposition of just such a reunion.

Katie leaned towards her. 'Perhaps you feel I've no right to seek out my daughter in this way?'

'Why ... why no,' she faltered. 'I ... I don't think that at all.'

'You're not well!' Katie got to her feet. 'I'm so sorry. How selfish of me to burden you with my troubles ... I ...'

'No, no!' Ann put out a hand. 'Don't go, please.'

'I must. Sister said no more than ten minutes.' She smiled and looked Ann over. 'I'm so pleased,' she said, moving slowly towards the door, 'that they didn't spoil your pretty face.'

'Katie!' Ann called after her, not wanting her to go, but already, the door was closing behind her.

She must have slept or dozed for a large part of that day, for the remainder was only a blur of comings and goings. It was quite dark when Iain next appeared accompanied by the night nurse, who pulled the blind before putting on the light.

'Your mother phoned about twenty minutes ago,' he told her.

Ann started. 'She knows then?'

'No, no. She phoned your flat, not here.' He tutted. 'Don't you remember, you asked me to ask Helga ...?'

'Of course. How silly of me.'

He held out a piece of paper. 'That's the number of her hotel. I ...'

'So I could phone her back!' Ann interrupted.

'Do you think you're well enough?'

'Of course I am,' she answered testily. 'I keep telling you I'm well enough to go home.'

Ignoring her last remark, Iain turned to the nurse. 'Bring a wheelchair will you?'

'Why can't I use the portable phone?' Ann asked as soon as the nurse had left the room.

'Because it's a pay phone,' he replied patiently. 'Wouldn't your mother want to know why you were in a call box?'

'Of course. How silly of me,' she said, for the second time in minutes.

The nurse reappeared just then with a wheelchair and after moving it up close to the bed, looked expectantly at Iain.

'Thank you, Nurse. That will be all.' Once she had gone, he stood back a few paces and folded his arms. 'Now. If you just hop into that chair, I'll wheel you down to the phone in Sister's office.'

What was he thinking of, Ann wondered? She could barely turn over without assistance, and here he was, expecting her to 'hop' as he put it, unaided into the wheelchair. She eased herself forward, her hands behind her and very gradually managed to swing her legs over the side of the bed. The effort was more painful than she could have imagined. Tears pricked at her eyes and she felt the room and everything in it, begin to swim around her.

In one swift movement Iain had pushed the wheelchair aside and was there beside her, his hands firmly supporting her shoulders. 'You little fool,' he murmured.

'Perhaps now you'll see you're not fit to go home.'

Anger flared within her then just as quickly dispersed when he put a hand on her head and held her near him. She could do nothing to stop the tears coursing unashamedly down her cheeks.

They were not tears of self-pity, she told herself, but simply an unshedding of all her pent-up emotions—her longing to reveal her identity without the risk of harming her adoptive mother; the reluctance of letting James down; the shock of the accident and not least, Iain's apparent revived affection for Helga.

Not until she had calmed herself did he make any move. Then very gently, his hands on her shoulders, he held her away from the support of his body and looked down at her. 'Would you like me to phone your mother?'

'Oh no. I ...'

'Your voice,' he interrupted. 'She'll know you've been crying.'

Suddenly, all the fight went out of her. 'Could you,' she said, 'without alarming her?'

He took her request as an acceptance of his offer. 'White lies were intended for such occasions,' he told her, lifting her legs back onto the bed and lowering her carefully down against the pillows. 'Just leave it with me.'

Once she was left alone again in the room, she was filled with a sense of peace. It was as if Iain had set out to show her that events would have to be allowed to take their own course, that she was no longer in full control.

When he returned he remained at the foot of the bed. 'I've told her you're staying at my place, that I've put you to bed early and you'll phone her tomorrow.'

'Oh you haven't! What did she say?'

'She seemed a little taken aback until I told her I'd met her sister-in-law and that seemed to make it all right.'

'But she'll be sure to phone Aunt Brenda

now to find out what's going on.'

'Of course she will, but I beat her to it. Remember, you gave us your aunt's phone number.'

'Oh!' Ann put her hands to her face. 'What will my poor mother think?'

'But you *are* staying at my place and I *have* put you to bed early.' There was a wicked gleam in his eyes. 'She said to tell you that your sister's had the first of her tests today.'

'Anything else?'

'She sent her love. Now, before I forget, Helga is anxious to visit you. All right if I bring her in tomorrow?'

'Helga?' Just to hear him speak her name took away all the pleasure of his presence. 'Yes ... yes I suppose so.'

'Is there anything you'd like her to fetch you from the flat?'

Ann pondered. 'Yes ... yes there is something ... something I'd rather was here with me,' and she went on to explain what she wanted.

Her sleep that night was broken by long hours of wakefulness when her mind became strangely, crystal clear. One by one she faced up to her dilemmas, and only after reaching a decision did she put them from her mind. She could no longer flounder on the way she had been doing.

TWELVE

Next day, when Aunt Brenda arrived during the afternoon visiting hour, Ann set about tackling her first hurdle.

'I want you to tell me everything you know about my mother's accident,' she told her as soon as she was seated.

'You don't want to be bothered with that now,' her aunt protested.

'Oh but I do.'

'Just forget it and tell me about this Mr Kirk. Are you and he ...?'

'Let's leave Mr Kirk out of this. Now you've *got* to tell me about my mother's accident,' Ann pleaded. 'It could be important.'

'Oh well!' Aunt Brenda shuffled further into the bedside chair. 'It's that long since, I suppose it can't do any harm. It was just after Iris and Frank were married when the accident occurred.' She sighed and shook her head. 'The driver of the other car was killed. Iris, your mother, was charged with manslaughter.'

Ann couldn't suppress the gasp which escaped her lips.

'Wait a bit. Wait a bit!' Aunt Brenda put up a hand. 'She was no more guilty than you or me, but it was weeks before a witness came forward.'

'How ... how did she cope?'

'She didn't. That's the whole point. You have to remember,' she added hastily, 'I wasn't on the scene at this time, so I only know all this from what John has told me.'

'Go on,' Ann urged.

'Well.' She paused. 'She had a nervous breakdown. It was bad I believe, for she was in that place in York, that private place, for months.'

'The Haven?' Ann prompted.

'That's it.' She stretched her legs out

and looked down at them. 'Sad business. She never has got over the shame of it.'

'Sad, yes. But why the shame?'

'Oh, things've changed since those days. Quite respectable to have a nervous complaint these days. It wasn't then.' She shook her head. 'By Jove it wasn't.'

Realization began to dawn on Ann. 'I see,' she whispered. 'I see.'

'Not all of it you don't,' Aunt Brenda said.

'How do you mean?'

'I don't know if I've not already told you more than I should.'

'Then let me try and guess the rest.'

Her aunt looked at her sharply. 'What d'you mean?'

'Isn't this why, for all these years, she's been opposed and afraid of any contact with my natural mother?'

'You know then?'

'That she was a nurse at The Haven— yes. You almost told me as much that day out on the farm.'

'I should have learnt to keep my big mouth shut.' Again she looked sharply at her niece. 'You'll not let on you know any of this?'

It was some time before Ann replied. 'It's gone too far to retreat now. Besides ...'

'You don't know what you're doing. You ...'

'Believe me I do.'

'You can't,' Aunt Brenda said earnestly. 'Just listen will you, while I try to explain.'

Ann made no reply, but leant back on her pillows and looked steadily at her aunt.

'When your parents picked you out from the Rescue Home, they knew *nothing* about your background.' She leaned forward and gazed at her niece. 'In next to no time, Iris was besotted with you. Then, perhaps you know, a few details are disclosed. No names, just a bit of background.'

'Like the fact that my mother was a psychiatric nurse in York?'

'Just that! So there was Iris, who'd struggled to put her breakdown behind her, suddenly confronted with it all again—through you!'

Ann shook her head at the irony of it all but said nothing.

'She was so afraid, even then, that through your mother you would one day find out about her breakdown, that she very nearly gave you up.'

Ann smiled. 'I'm glad she didn't. But don't you see, Aunt, she's been worrying all these years over nothing.'

'No, no child. You don't understand.'

'Do you suppose for one minute, I think any worse of my mother, who for twenty-six years gave me all she had, just because I now know she once suffered a nervous breakdown?'

'Iris used to worry that this nurse, your *real* mother, if you were to find her, would poison your mind against her.'

'Out of hundreds of patients it's unlikely she'll even remember her.' She looked into her aunt's troubled face and said softly. 'Besides, Katie wouldn't know how to begin to poison anyone's mind about anything.' She shut her eyes, suddenly exhausted.

'Katie?' she heard her aunt say.

'My *real* mother.'

'You've found her then?'

'Yes. I've found her.'

Aunt Brenda gasped but said nothing.

A great sadness filled Ann that over the years her mother should have known such torment and all because of the awful stigma attached to mental illness.

'Do you want to tell me about Katie?' her aunt asked finally.

'Not just now. Perhaps some other time.'

'What'll we tell Iris when she phones today? She was very suspicious about this Mr Kirk when ...'

'We'll tell her the truth,' Ann intervened. 'That I've had a slight bump and they're keeping me in for a few days.'

'Well, I suppose you know what you're

doing. Those flowers.' Ann had seen her aunt peering at the card. 'I gather they're from James. Has he been in to see you?'

'No. Nor will he be coming.'

'Why's that? Is he away somewhere?'

'Not yet, but he soon will be.' Ann went on to explain about his new job.

'Bit far from here to London.' There was a note of hope in her voice.

'Which is why,' Ann told her, 'we felt it a good time to end our relationship.'

'Oh well.' Aunt Brenda tried hard but couldn't hide the relief in her voice. 'There's plenty more fish in the sea.'

Ann had written the letter to James during the morning and had been strangely comforted by the closing of that chapter of her life. She had never loved him—she knew that with certainty now.

Her aunt had not been gone long when a young nurse burst in carrying an overnight case belonging to Ann. Dumping it unceremoniously on the bed she unloosed the catch and threw back the lid. 'This has just come up from the porter's desk. You can have one of your own nighties on now.'

'Oh.' What had happened to Helga, Ann wondered. 'I was expecting someone with it. Was there no no message?'

'Can't have been,' the young nurse replied, 'or it would've come up with the case. Unless this is it.' She held out a plain brown envelope from among the nightdresses.

Ann took it from her. 'No, that's something else, something I asked for.' She slipped it into her locker drawer, relieved that Iain had not forgotten to ask Helga to put it in.

When later, Sister got her out of bed and allowed her to take a few paces round the room, Ann was surprised to discover how jelly-like her legs were and how light-headed she felt after less than forty-eight hours in bed. Nevertheless, she ventured to ask, 'Do you think Mr Kirk will let me go home soon?' She was feeling a little sore that he hadn't looked in yet today.

'I couldn't say, Doctor Davis. He's in theatre all day today so ...' She shrugged her shoulders as much as to say 'You can write today off for a start'.

It was arranged that Ann would phone her mother after supper when she was most likely to be back in her hotel. She was only half-way through the light meal when the door was pushed open.

'I've a surprise for you,' Sister told her, and stood back to allow a sun-tanned woman in a striking blue suit to enter.

'Mum!'

'Ann, my child!' In one swift move Iris Davis was across the small room pulling her daughter's head close to her ample bosom. 'Thank God you're all right.' Then she held her away and searched her face. 'You are all right, aren't you?'

Ann winced for the movement was jolting and painful. 'I am, really. But what ... what are you doing here?'

'Wonderful news, child. Wonderful.' Iris's eyes were bright with tears as she let go her hold on Ann and sat on the edge of the bed. 'I'm going to be a grandmother.' Now she was laughing and crying all at once.

'How ... how do you mean, Mum?'

'Why Jane of course! She's pregnant.'

'But ... but I thought ...'

'So did we all, my dear, even Jane.' Her brows puckered and she put a hand to Ann's head. 'You look so pale. You sure you're all right?'

'Yes, really. Now tell me about Jane.'

Her mother opened her bag and began rummaging in it. 'There!' She brought out a tiny package. 'She sent you this.'

Nestling in the tissue paper was a brooch in the finest bone china.

'It's a Bermuda Lily,' her mother told her.

Ann felt her eyes smart as she held it in her palm. 'Tell me about her, Mum.'

'Well.' Iris shook her head in bewilderment. 'When we arrived yesterday, the specialist spent a long time questioning her then infuriated poor Jane by saying he would commence with a pregnancy test.'

'Go on.'

'You know the rest.' Iris clasped her hands together. 'It was positive.'

'But surely ...'

'Well, you know how irregular she's always been. My dear, if you'd seen her face!' She closed her eyes briefly. 'All she wanted was to get back to Rick. She was lucky enough to get a seat on a stand-by.'

'It's kind of hard to believe.'

'As soon as I'd seen her off to the airport, I took a train up here.' A long sigh escaped her. 'I phoned your aunt on arrival ... and here I am.'

The full impact of her surroundings seemed to hit Iris then and Ann watched the shoulders sag, the sparkle evaporate and all the joy go out of her mother.

'When Mr Kirk phoned me last evening, I wondered what on earth you were up to.' She shook her head, a sombre expression on her face. 'I think anything would have been better than this.'

'Oh Mum.' Ann laughed softly. 'But I'm all right.'

'But the accident. What if you're accused ...'

'Stop it, Mum!' Ann was alarmed by the glassy, faraway look in her mother's eyes.

The door opened just then and Sister came in carrying a tray of tea. 'I thought your mother would be ready for a cup, Doctor Davis, travelling all that way from London.'

The interruption was well timed for after Sister had gone, Ann watched her mother gradually unwind, as seated now in an armchair alongside the bed, she sipped the warm tea.

Despite numerous rehearsals of just how she would begin to tell her mother about Katie, it was some time before Ann could get out the words. 'There's something I want to tell you, Mum. Something that's come to light since you went away'

It was almost as if Iris knew what was coming, for without looking at her daughter, she nodded her head. 'Tell me, child,' she whispered.

Bit by bit, Ann let the story of her search unfold.

A gasp of anguish escaped Iris's lips at the point where Ann related how she'd been called out to Katie when she'd collapsed.

'And now?' she probed in a muffled voice, her face buried in her hands.

'She's a patient on this ward.'

The groan that followed seemed to go right through Ann.

'So she knows who you are then?' her mother asked.

'No. She doesn't know who I am. Not yet.' She waited for this to sink in before going on. 'But I know what happened to you all those years ago.'

Very slowly, Iris took her hands from her

face. 'You do?' she asked, utter despair in her expression. She sat forward and leaned her arms across the bed.

'Yes,' Ann said softly, taking hold of her mother's hands. 'I know about your accident and about the breakdown.'

'But how ... how ...?'

'Aunt Brenda. I made her tell me.'

'And ... and you're not ashamed?' She felt her mother's eyes upon her.

'Why should I be? Saddened yes, that you've felt you had this terrible cross to bear. But ashamed—of you? Never!'

There was a gentle knocking on the door just then.

'Come in,' Ann called, still holding onto her mother's hands.

'Oh, I'm so sorry, Doctor Davis.' It was Katie Sykes. '... I thought you'd be on your own.'

'Please. Don't go.' Ann's heart was pounding thunderously inside her chest. 'I'd like you to meet my mother.'

'Oh!' Katie smiled, looking a little

abashed and letting the door close behind her, edged into the room.

'Mum. This is Katie Sykes,' Ann managed, her mouth dry. 'Katie, this is my mother, Iris Davis.'

At sight of the frail woman in night attire, Iris had risen to her feet. She stood now behind her chair, her gaze transfixed on Katie who was extending a hand towards her.

'Mrs Davis.' Katie's thin face lit up. 'It's lovely to meet you.' She half turned towards Ann. 'Your daughter here is a marvellous doctor you know.'

'Please ... please sit down,' Iris said, after briefly clasping the extended hand. Then very slowly, her eyes never leaving Katie's face, she made her way round to the chair at the other side of the bed. 'You ... you don't remember me then?'

'I'm sorry.' Katie put her head to one side. 'Should I ...?'

'You ... you nursed me once at ... at The Haven.'

'Did I?' Katic smiled. 'You must forgive me. We doctors and nurses,' she looked towards Ann, 'I'm sure your daughter will agree with me—we see so many patients you know, it's difficult to remember.'

Ann felt she was on a stage, watching and listening, waiting for her cue. Then she felt Iris's eyes upon her. 'Tell her' they seemed to be saying. 'Tell her'.

The plain brown envelope was just inside her locker drawer. Raising the flap, she slid out the yellowing form and unfolding it, held it towards Katie so that she could read the neat black handwriting.

There was absolute silence in the room, broken only by the trundling of a kitchen trolley in the corridor outside. Somewhere a telephone was ringing, then that too was silenced.

'My birth certificate,' Ann heard herself say in a voice choked with emotion.

Katie had taken hold of the certificate and was staring at it as if in disbelief at what was written there.

The waiting was unbearable. Ann's hands were clenched on top of the bedclothes and she pressed them firmly down in an effort to still them. She dare not look to the left where her adoptive mother sat, but was deeply grateful when she felt the warmth of her hand cover hers and squeeze it reassuringly.

Finally, Katie's eyes left the piece of paper she held and sought Ann's. 'You ... you can't mean ...?'

Slowly, Ann nodded, then watched as the thin face took on an expression of wonderment, eyes sparkling, mouth widening, like a child experiencing her first Christmas. Dropping the certificate into her lap, Katie's hands reached out and clasped Ann's free one. For what seemed an eternity she didn't speak, but gazed at Ann as if allowing time for the truth to dawn.

'I knew you were special,' she whispered. 'All along I knew. But this ... this is more than I ever dreamed.'

Tears blinded Ann and there was nothing she could say.

Then it was as if Katie had only just remembered the woman, who for twenty-six years had been a mother to her child. She reached out a hand towards her. 'You've done a wonderful job,' she told her. 'Wonderful. How can I ever begin to thank ...'

'Don't try,' Iris interrupted. 'Ann has brought nothing but joy to our lives.' Then she too reached out and took hold of Katie's hand so that the three were linked, bringing about such happiness that Ann felt her heart would burst with pride.

Much later, after all three finally parted, Ann fell into an exhausted sleep.

She awoke with a suddenness to hear someone calling her name. Dragging herself from the depths of a deep sleep, she opened her eyes to find Iain Kirk standing in a pool of soft light at the foot of her bed.

'Hi. I thought you'd never wake up.'

Still sleepy, she rubbed her eyes. 'Is it ... is it morning?'

He chuckled softly. 'Not quite. It's a quarter to midnight. I didn't want to go home without seeing you.'

His words brought a thrill of pleasure to Ann. She put a hand to her hair self-consciously.

'There's no need to do that,' he told her. 'You look lovely just as you are.' He came round to stand beside her. 'Did you get your case?'

'Yes ... yes thank you.' His nearness disturbed her. 'But what happened to Helga? I thought she was going to look in.'

Again he chuckled softly. 'Helga has flown, my love.'

She started. What was that he had called her? And what was that he had said about Helga? 'How ... how do you mean? Flown.'

'Back to the wilds of Northumberland.'

'But surely ...?'

'She saw something on T.V. about an oil-slick up there. Went off leaving a scribbled note about Gavin needing her to help rescue the birds.'

Ann was puzzled by what sounded to her like a note of satisfaction in Iain's voice. She tried to read the expression on his face but the shadows made it impossible. 'You ... you don't sound very upset.'

'Upset! Quite the contrary—I'm highly delighted.'

'But ... I thought ...'

'What exactly did you think?'

'Well. That you and her ... Oh! You must know what I thought. She was your ex-fiancée when all is said and done.'

'Which is exactly why I did what I did,' he reasoned tenderly, perching on the edge of her bed. 'You saw how depressed she was becoming after failing that interview.'

'But helping her find work was one thing. You didn't have to make her your personal secretary.'

'But don't you see, my love,' he

smoothed her cheek with the back of his hand, 'I couldn't have let anyone else employ her. I knew she'd go back to Gavin sooner or later.'

'You knew?' Strange things were happening to Ann and she wished Iain would go back to standing at the foot of the bed.

'Just as I knew from that first meeting at the airport, that you would one day be mine.' With his finger, he traced the line of her nose and round the curve of her mouth.

She was alarmed by the sensations shooting through her body. 'Please Iain,' she murmured, taking hold of his hand.

'You are quite right,' he told her, stooping and kissing the tip of her nose, 'we are behaving totally unprofessionally. You may go home tomorrow, Doctor Davis, and I shall take you myself.'

Later that same year, on the first Sunday in October, the early mist had cleared by noon to reveal a perfect, golden autumn day.

As the doorbell resounded through Ann's flat, she cast a last-minute look around. The table, with its centre-piece of the last of the summer roses, was laid for six. The oven was on low so that the baked potatoes and chicken and vegetable casserole, would cook slowly in her absence.

'Mmm.' Iain took her in his arms as she opened the door. 'I don't know what smells better.' He sniffed appreciatively. 'Your perfume or your cooking.'

'Come on, or we'll be keeping them waiting.' Banging the flat door shut, she took his hand and they descended the stairs like a couple of playful children.

In a short while, the blue TR7 had purred its way the short distance to the pinewoods and was pulling in behind an old Ford.

Tumbling out, Ann went straight to the open passenger door of the car in front and stooping, kissed the cheek of the woman sitting there.

'You're here then,' Henry Sykes announced from behind the steering-wheel. He opened his door and stepped out.

'I hope you've not been waiting long,' Ann said earnestly.

'Not more than a couple of minutes,' Katie told her, while Ann helped her to her feet.

'Good morning Henry, Katie,' Iain called, strolling up. 'Where are the lads? You've surely not left them behind?'

'No such luck.' Henry chortled, falling into step beside Iain. 'They've gone ahead,' he waved his stick, 'in search of conkers.'

'However do you manage, Ann,' Katie asked as she linked her arm through her daughter's, 'to have six of us for lunch and still find time to come for a walk?'

'But I've little else to do in my off-duty hours.'

'You've been saying that ever since I

came out of hospital,' Katie objected. 'I don't know how I'd ever have managed without you.'

'Nonsense.' Ann held back an overhanging branch.

'It's true. And as for your mother—I shan't ever be able to repay her for all she did that first week I was home from hospital.'

Ann laughed. 'I think she might still be here if Dad hadn't begun to feel neglected.'

'I've often thought ... it can't have been easy for Iris ... having me appear on the scene after all those years. She's hardly changed you know.'

'So you did remember her?'

Katie paused in her tracks. 'Oh yes—not her name—but her face.' She sighed then. 'Just look at that. I'd quite forgotten how lovely these woods could be in autumn.'

Shafts of sunlight filtered through gaps in the tall trees transforming the drenching dew so that the undergrowth was a glistening silvery gossamer. Trailing black-berry briars covered with red and yellow leaves, made fine patches of colour interwoven with the dark green foliage. The air was heavy with a damp, woody smell.

Henry and Iain were now well ahead and the only sound was a bird singing somewhere above their heads. Ann watched Katie as she stood there quite still, before raising a hand and brushing it across her cheeks.

'What is it?' she asked urgently.

'What is it,' Katie's voice, barely more than a whisper, was choked with emotion. 'It's just ... it's just that I've never known such happiness.' She smiled at her daughter through her tears.

Ann put an arm about her. 'Oh, Mother. No-one deserves it more than you.'

Then the moment was lost as a cracking of twigs and high-pitched squeals of delight heralded the arrival of Katie's boys.

'Go on then.' Ben pushed Paul forward. 'Ask her.'

Ann waited, amused at this pretence of shyness.

'Paul wants to know,' Ben began boldly, 'if he saves up, can he go to Kenya with you at Christmas?'

'And you!' Paul accused. 'You said you wanted to go as well.'

'I never,' Ben protested, kicking the toe of his shoe against a fallen log.

'Boys. Boys.' Their mother began to make for a bench. 'Apart from the enormous cost, I think there's something you don't quite understand.'

Ann smiled and walking a few paces away, decided to leave Katie to explain.

'Ann and Iain are going to Kenya for their honeymoon,' she heard. 'Now honeymoons are very private affairs so ...'

Later that day, when all six of them were gathered round the table in her flat, Ann let her eyes travel from one to the other. She hoped she would be forgiven if her gaze rested longer on her mother's face, for had it not been for her existence,

Ann may never have come to Hargate, and that was now something she couldn't bare to contemplate.

This Large Print Book for the Partially sighted, who cannot read normal print, is published under the auspices of

THE ULVERSCROFT FOUNDATION

THE ULVERSCROFT FOUNDATION

. . . we hope that you have enjoyed this Large Print Book. Please think for a moment about those people who have worse eyesight problems than you . . . and are unable to even read or enjoy Large Print, without great difficulty.

You can help them by sending a donation, large or small to:

**The Ulverscroft Foundation,
1, The Green, Bradgate Road,
Anstey, Leicestershire, LE7 7FU,
England.**

or request a copy of our brochure for more details.

The Foundation will use all your help to assist those people who are handicapped by various sight problems and need special attention.

Thank you very much for your help.